# Chester Midshipmouse

# Chester Midshipmouse

*Susan Weisberg*

**Illustrations by R. Leigh Anderson**

ISBN-13: 9780999057940
ISBN-10: 0999057944
Library of Congress Control Number: 2017957039
Brass Button Books, Ocean View, NJ

# Preface

❧

BEHIND THE MASSIVE GRAY STONE walls of Bancroft Hall, at the United States Naval Academy, where young men and women train to become naval officers, battalions of mice also train to become military leaders. These furry creatures follow rules and traditions similar to those of the human midshipmen in the dormitory rooms of the sprawling building, whom they are pleased to visit from time to time.

This is the story of Chester—a midshipmouse.

# Acknowledgments

✣

MANY THANKS TO THOSE WHO aided in bringing Chester's story to print, particularly the early readers of the manuscript: Susan McPheeters; Angela Gkonos; and my dear ninety-year-old mother, Dorothy Gkonos, who still corrects my grammar.

Thank you, professional editor and friend, Katharine Cluverius Boak, for your invaluable expertise, encouragement, and advice. I am grateful also to author and friend Jennifer Shirk for the reams of savvy information willingly shared over many cups of coffee.

Utmost appreciation to our three children: Alex, your love of animal fantasy fiction as a child, knowledge of what makes pleasing narrative (I hope I've managed to provide a few of those moments in this book), and indispensable technical help in navigating the world of publishing and web marketing has made this your story as well. To our two midshipmen, who read bits; made corrections; and answered questions by phone, by text, and in person even when you were supposed to be studying or polishing your shoes to a bright shine—thank you for willingly sharing your life. It's amazing how many of your memories were captured on scraps of paper napkins in Annapolis restaurants. Bryan, you began this journey, named the mouse, and shared the tales that became legend. And Ben (who really did have an unbelievable meet-up with a mouse, but that's an anecdote for the next story), thanks for always being *wise*. Special gratitude to my husband, Bill, for sending funny, uplifting cards to our plebes and for believing this story from day one. You never doubted for a minute that a little tawny-furred mouse named Chester, along with his band of rodents, were really training to become midshipmice behind the noble gray stone walls of Bancroft Hall (and they really are). Thank you for being extraordinarily patient, as well as an ardent fan, promoter, and supporter.

To my incredible artist and illustrator, Rachael Anderson. This book wouldn't be the same without your creative talent and ability to work "magic." Thank you for your willingness to pore over a mind-numbing number of photos in order to create the midshipmice and their world just as they really are! How did you do that? It has been an enjoyable collaboration. With gratitude also to Wendy Mays of WendyLynn and Co., Children's Book Illustrators, for your professional support.

To the three great roommates of "the Bastion"—Bryan, Patrick, and Murphy—whose antics approached mythical proportions and who bear an uncanny resemblance to Chester, Dilly, and Ranger (except for the fur and tails): fair winds and following seas as you serve your country in jets, submarines, and helicopters.

To all the men and women graduates of the United States Naval Academy, who heeded the call and endured the rigors in order to earn the right to serve our nation and be called a naval or marine officer. This book is a love letter to you.

## CHAPTER 1

# The Mice at Home

❧

ABRUPT, FIRM PAW-STEPS ANNOUNCED THE arrival of five midshipmice in the living area of Chester's household, scattering three timid mice who were caught off guard by the intrusion. The military rodents were dressed in trim, dark suit jackets with brass buttons on the front, one or two gold stripes, and a star on the sleeves. Their long pink tails snapped smartly back and forth behind them as they stood straight and tall, not a whisker out of place, in front of Grandfather Nimitz. Chester crept closer, straining his ears to hear what they were saying, but their conversation was calm and quiet. Other young mice stopped scampering about and paused to stare, some caught midchew, their long front teeth hanging out.

All about the floorboards, tucked haphazardly into nooks and crannies, comfy nests made of clumps of string and fluff housed Chester's large family and their friends. On most nights the young mice nosed about searching for crumbs or wandered aimlessly in the warm, compact ceiling and wall spaces of the building. The adults scurried in and out, carrying bits of food in their mouths, chewing contentedly, or dumping their finds into a big heap for others to share. The life of an ordinary house mouse was a random contented one, except on a few occasions. Chester thought it could be a bit boring.

The presence of the midshipmice startled all the rodents. They were only sent into the house-mouse areas of Bancroft Hall when there was a *situation*, which wasn't very often.

"What's up?" a young mouse questioned.

"I smell something fishy," another muttered.

"Something's amiss, buddy," Theo said in an aside to his friend Chester as he brushed by, pushing a bit of pizza crust with his snout.

Chester held himself still, watching, his forepaws folded across his chest. Even Chester's mother, who had been trotting back and forth gathering crumbs and morsels for their next meal, stopped when she saw the uniformed mice. Mama sat back on her tail, forepaws in front of her light, furry belly, pink nose sniffing the air for trouble. She was anxious but did not want to frighten the young ones. Chester's papa rubbed his grand snout in a casual manner but moved in to hear what was being said. He glanced at Mama a few times through his glasses to reassure her.

Chester hunched down to the floor to assess the strangers, his round, black glistening eyes noticing every detail—the close-cropped hair between their upright ears and their impeccable uniforms. They clutched their black-brimmed white hats closely to their lean flanks under muscular forepaws. Chester snuck a peek at his own clean fur and licked a tuft that was sticking out. Absently he wet his paws with his tongue, smoothed the tawny fur between his ears with quick swipes, and then glanced down to see if his belly stuck out as he twitched his tail into a more precise position. What would he look like in one of those uniforms?

The midshipmice were just a bit older than Chester, but they were confident and talked smoothly to his grandfather. Perhaps they had brought really important news, like a cat on the premises. Now that would be exciting! Chester pictured himself with a long, shiny sword slicing off the enemy cat's whiskers one by one, poking its nose as it backed out of the room, hissing in fear.

Only he didn't own a sword.

He had once found a large silver safety pin and had figured out how to release the pointy end from the protective cover. That could come in handy. He wondered where it was. *Better look for it,* he thought with a little reminder to himself.

Grandfather finished the conversation with a nod. The five midshipmice saluted smartly; turned on their long, pointy heels; and left as abruptly as they had come, making sure to greet the adult mice politely, calling them "sir" or "ma'am" as they exited.

Immediately the older mice crowded around Chester's grandfather, pushing their whiskered noses in close, asking questions with high-pitched chatters and squeaks. Grandfather held up his paws to shush them, patting the air calmly. He moved to the Great Hourglass that stood prominently at the end of the Gathering Hall. The hourglass was an egg timer filled with sand at the bottom and used in gathering hall meetings. When it was flipped, the sand would pour from the top to the bottom in three minutes, which was about the normal mouse attention span. Grandfather rested a paw on the lower glass globe, commanding attention.

"All is well, all is well," he reassured the horde of mice beginning to gather. "They were only here to report the sighting of a water rat in the basin."

Chester heard a few utterances such as "Eek" and "What next?"

The mice called anything that swam, had fur, and was not a mouse a water rat. They hated rats with a passion, but what the midshipmice had actually reported spotting was a river otter, which was far more dangerous to Chester and his family because river otters were known to eat small rodents.

"The water rat has been spied on two different occasions near the waterfront. One of those times it was in the river basin that houses the human sailing vessels. All mice are to stay clear of those areas until further notice. The midshipmice have organized patrols for our safety," Grandfather explained.

As the old mouse spoke these words, Chester lifted his snout. A little tingle of something in the air tickled his nostrils. Out of the corner of his eye, he saw Theo stop nibbling the tomato layer from his bread crust. They glanced at each other. Several other mice sniffed the air, pointing their noses this way and that. Grandfather paused, at alert.

The midshipmice burst back into the communal area, alarming everyone. "*Fire!*" they yelled.

Two of the midshipmice grabbed the Great Hourglass that they had spotted moments earlier while speaking with Grandfather. They rushed away on their hind legs, each hoisting an end in their forepaws.

The other three naval mice pushed the horde of household mice away from the faint smell of smoke, scattering the frantic creatures as they urged them to evacuate.

"Run!" shrieked Mama.

Chester followed Grandfather, who was in slow pursuit of the uniformed mice. Furry bodies scampered past in the opposite direction, shoving and tripping over whipping tails in their haste to get away. Chester had to use his nose as a wedge and shoulders as a block to withstand the tide of fleeing mice. His sensitive ears were getting bumped, folded backward, and squashed in the stampede. He saw Grandfather trot to his nest and pull a thick blue square blanket from his sleeping area.

The five midshipmice were now gathered around a pile of fluff next to a beam, calling each other by name. They were examining Pip's nest.

The longest midshipmouse, who was tallest on his hind legs, yelled to the others before he turned and disappeared into the dark, "Electrical! Extinguish!"

The uniformed mice sent their hats, which they called covers, skimming across the floor, pushed back the sleeves on their furry forearms, and pulled away clumps of smoldering fluff. Puffs of smoke billowed into the dark. With quick movements, the most muscular rodent picked up a metal nail lying on the floor.

"Do it, Bingo!" a midshipmouse named Zigzag shouted.

With a mighty swing, he smashed the top of the hourglass dome. Charlie and Zigzag hefted the remaining globe filled with sand and poured it over the smoldering nest.

"Blanket!" Charlie ordered.

Grandfather tossed his blue square to Chester, who scurried toward the military mice, trying to be as efficient with his movements as they were. Chester delivered the blanket and skittered backward on all fours as the midshipmice dropped it over the debris they had pulled from Pip's nest to finish smothering the burning embers.

Chester eased back toward Grandfather, who stood watch at the entrance to make sure none of the household mice returned to the area until all was clear.

From the other end of the dim living space, the tall midshipmouse reappeared, pushing a roll of black sticky tape like a wheel across the floor.

"How far did you have to go to find it?" Bingo called out.

"Not far. Went to Twenty-Seventh Company's fire station and secured their supply."

The tall mouse picked at the end of the tape with his claws and gnawed off a short length. The midshipmice probed and isolated a wire from the wall right next to Pip's nest, which had been chewed through and was frayed.

Chester heard Grandfather mutter under his breath, "It would be Pip."

Charlie and Bingo carefully held the plastic-coated ends of the wire on either side of the break and pushed them together until they touched, twisting to mesh the loose ends. The tall midshipmouse wound the black tape tightly around the junction and pressed the end to seal.

Chester was in awe.

"Grandfather," he whispered with his deep voice, "how did they know what to do?"

"Midshipmice are trained to be aware of their surroundings at all times. They practice *situational awareness.* Did you see, Chester, how they knew the hourglass full of sand was nearby?"

"Yes." Chester was thinking rapidly. "But how did they know how to put out the fire?"

"Rigorous training. Damage control and double *E.* They learned to use sand, not water, to put out this type of fire in double *E.*"

"Double *E?*"

"Electrical emergencies...a class all midshipmice are required to take in their second or third season."

"They fixed the wire too."

"All midshipmice can do that. Imagine what would have happened if the Bancroft Hall alarm had gone off."

Chester knew exactly what would have happened. The jarring, ringing sound would have gone on and on, irritating their sensitive ears. The household would have scattered. At the worst they would have fled for their lives from a raging fire. He grimaced, thankful that had never happened in his short life. At the least, a large human would have come nosing around on his hands and knees, invading their space, scattering belongings and sweeping out their stores, looking for the source of the alarm. Their peaceful life would have been impacted for weeks.

"It's not just us, Chester," Grandfather continued. "If the alarm bells had rung, all the human midshipmen would have been awakened from their sleep and sent at a run outdoors in the cold and dark, standing in formation in their companies for hours. They would lose valuable sleep. It is our duty to protect them during the night."

This concept had never occurred to Chester. Formation? Companies? What were the humans doing? Later he would ask Grandfather more about what those words meant.

The five midshipmice brushed off their coats, flicked fluff from the sleeves, picked up their covers, and approached Grandfather.

"Sir," said the mouse named Zigzag, "I believe the fire is resolved. Maybe you should remove the burnt-nest material from the area. Sorry about the hourglass."

"We can replace an hourglass. Thank you for your quick thinking," Grandfather replied.

The household mice returned from hiding once they realized that the fire alarm bells had not rung. They grouped hesitantly about Grandfather as he again conferred with the midshipmice. Chester watched as the five prepared to exit. After the harrowing emergency, they still spoke with calm respect to the adult mice. Chester realized they saw it as their duty and was pleased that he too had been able to help, even if in a small way.

Order was soon restored: the glass shards and blackened fragments were swept away with long-handled toothbrushes, Pip got a good talking to after his mama pried open his jaws to see if his tongue had been fried while chewing the wires, and the adult mice went gratefully about their usual business.

Several of the very young mice clamored to know more about the midshipmice. Some had seen them before but knew very little about them.

"Who were those rodents?"

"Why did they have stripes on their sleeves?"

"Where do they live?"

"Why did they salute you, Grandfather?"

The old mouse smiled. "They did not need to salute because I am retired and out of uniform, but they did so out of respect. My rank was rear admiral in the Mouse Navy."

An adolescent mouse snickered somewhere nearby, wiggling his hind end.

"A rank that gave me two stars on my uniform," Grandfather continued. "Would you like to see my coat?"

There were nods and shouts in the affirmative. Even though he knew the story, Chester was suddenly hungry to hear more about Grandfather's history.

"Were you a midshipmouse?" Chester asked to get Grandfather started.

"Yes. Long before you were born, I was appointed to train as a midshipmouse. I was placed in Sixth Company, and a fine group of rodents that was!"

The juvenile mice began to crowd closer, asking more questions. Grandfather pretended to hold them back with his paws, but Chester could tell he was enjoying the attention by the smile on his gray snout.

"If you sit patiently, I will tell you the story of the midshipmice of Bancroft Hall."

Grandfather moved slowly to his belongings, retrieved his carefully folded black suit jacket from his neatly arranged nest, shrugged himself into it, and fastened the buttons. The coat still fit nicely, though it was a bit loose across the shoulders where two stars and an anchor rested on the gold boards extending out from the collar. Returning to the mass of mice jumbled about, he lowered himself down on his aged haunches and spoke quietly because the pink, furless babies were now asleep in their nests. His voice was strong and confident.

"There have been mice in Bancroft Hall for *more than* one hundred years," he proudly told Chester and the other young ones who had gathered to sit at his feet.

"I think the Old Buck's been here the whole time," Chester's cousin Pip whispered behind his paw.

Chester stuck his short elbow in Pip's side to hush him. He was still annoyed that Pip had chewed a wire in the wall while grinding down his long front teeth, nearly getting them all burnt to a crisp.

Grandfather's fur was graying, yet still held golden lights. Chester smoothed his own shiny, tawny coat, his round pink ears perked and attentive.

He asked in his quiet, deep voice, "Grandfather, who gets to wear the blue and gold?"

Grandfather Nimitz looked at Chester with a certain sparkle in his eye. "Very few. Only those who are *selected*."

There were sighs. Light filtered through cracks in the floorboard of the narrow space where they were gathered. Some of the restless young scurried away, while other juvenile mice remained listening. Chester ignored those who were sniffing absently or jostling him to slip out of the group. Grandfather had his full attention.

"Why do we have midshipmice?" a young, reedy voice called out.

"Your forebearers—and there have been a lot of them," Grandfather began with a little chuckle, "made their home here as soon as the first stones of Bancroft Hall were put into place. Ever since, the mice have been observing and sharing with the human students who come to live and train here."

"Why were the humans living here? Didn't they want to live in their own houses?" another asked.

"This great building was constructed as a dormitory, a place for the humans to live together while they went to school *and* learned to become naval officers. In the very beginning, a smart and brave rodent set a challenge to the house mice. He said we also should be trained to serve and protect our own just as the humans do."

"Why?"

"Because from the time the mice moved in, there were threats to their peaceful existence. Other creatures, including a black rat off a ship in the harbor, attempted to infiltrate and take over."

All the mice shuddered at the mention of a rat—especially a black ship rat, the most fierce and aggressive breed of all rats.

*Rattus rattus,* thought Chester with a grimace.

"Through his leadership, that first courageous mouse saved the household rodents from grave danger," Grandfather continued.

"What was his name?" squeaked a young female.

"His name was George, in honor of the human who brought specialized naval military training here from a distant city, a city called Philadelphia."

"*Philadelphia.*" Chester quietly tried out the new word. He shook his snout.

"Bancroft Hall is named after him. Many of the mice here are named after famous naval officers. Our George was a good soldier, a gentlemouse, a leader in the Naval Mouse Brigade, and a true warrior," Grandfather explained.

A high, perky voice shouted, "Are there any girls?"

Grandfather smiled. "Yes, Dixie, now there are female midship-mice, but you're too young yet."

The youthful mice stared.

"How did the Naval Mouse Academy get started, Grandfather?" Chester was eager to hear his favorite part of the story.

"Only a pawful of courageous mice first dared to mimic the rig-orous human training they could see during daylight hours when normal house mice sleep. Those few mice studied the humans and ran and marched alongside them in the long grass, keeping out of sight and duplicating their every move. At night they crept into the young men's rooms to laboriously copy down the rules from their books. To keep up their strength, they borrowed bits of their food. They gave up sleep, gave up regular eating, and risked their lives in the daytime to develop the midshipmouse training program. They memorized songs and chants, practiced on drums, made bugles and parade rifles, and stitched up the first mouse uniforms just like the ones they saw the humans wear. The uniforms have hardly changed since." Grandfather grasped the cloth of his dark suit coat with both paws in display. "And that was when they began guard-ing the entry holes into Bancroft Hall, where the first squirrel was vanquished."

"Tree rats!" a mouse in the back muttered.

*Fuzzy-tailed rascals*, Chester thought with disdain.

All mice knew that squirrels would try to weasel their way in when the weather was cold. He shook his head and went on listen-ing to Grandfather Nimitz.

"Those brave and resourceful mice also patrolled the water-front, practiced their swimming, and made boats from the bits of floating debris they found in the water."

Chester's thoughts drifted. He tried to imagine those first swimming mice. He guessed that field mice were pretty good swimmers, but he was not. He had only waded a few times in the large puddle that formed after heavy rains on the red deck outside his home. The truth was, household mice generally stayed indoors. He wasn't even sure he could swim.

"At the end of that first summer, they paraded for all the house mice to see as they floated by in the river with sails billowing and showed the others what it meant to live with honor, duty, and courage and to be physically fit."

Chester pictured the boats in his mind, hulls skimming along the surface, bows pounding in the waves. A mouse in the front would cry out, "There she is, rodents. Annapolis town. Hoist the spinnaker; bring her 'round."

Anyway, this was how he imagined it would be. Chester had read a bit about boats. He would love to see one, but as a house mouse, there was rarely any reason to go outside. The mice had everything they needed right at their tail-tips, safe within the walls of the building. Chester wondered if he was missing something.

Grandfather lowered his voice, looking intently at the juvenile mice hanging on his every word, and spoke softly, "They envisioned a life so different from the way mice have always lived."

Straightening up, Grandfather raised his voice, the words echoing around the room and causing the young to jump. "Their training complete, these mice set a challenge to those who were confident and brave enough to accept: 'Live as we do for a season, learn to train other mice, and you will become the first officers of the Naval Mouse Brigade!'"

"How many took the challenge?" Pip called out.

"Oh, many started, but only a pawful finished."

"Why?"

"Because saying and doing are two different things."

Chester and his friends sat silently. Who among them might wish to take the challenge? Chester angled his whiskers and glanced around at the others, wondering what they were thinking.

Grandfather finished his story. "Soon a small group of mice were training every season. The numbers grew year by year. Word spread, and mice began to travel from far away, asking to be accepted. Today we have a large brigade of mice, some from far countries, being trained in one secure section of Bancroft Hall, a closed-off space that no house or field mouse is able to visit. The foreign mice take their training back to distant places, where they serve, protect, and train other rodents."

A new idea had been forming in Chester's mind. A piece of the story was missing. He squinted as he thought, whiskers twitching slightly. "Grandfather"—his voice was grave—"are we in danger from anything else?"

Grandfather paused. "Yes, Chester."

The furry young held their breath. A rodent gulped somewhere.

"Not all mice are good. Some groups of mice wish to overtake our building and our way of life for their own selfish purposes. They work in the blackest part of the night and attempt to infiltrate for their own nefarious designs. All they want to do is to eat and pillage. They have no regard for their fellow mouse. They seek to upset our peaceful lives and the balance we have achieved with the humans. Allowed to invade, they would overrun Bancroft Hall without check. There would be no order and no peace. Droppings would be everywhere. Food would become scarce, factions would form, and fighting would break out. It would be chaos."

The young mice glanced at each other with bulging eyes, mulling over this frightening piece of information.

"But *we* are safe here," Grandfather reassured, and the young mice exhaled with relief.

"Why do we never see the midshipmice?" Dixie asked.

"Because they remain separate until their training is complete, and we must stay out of their way and not distract them. They live very differently from you and me."

Chester marveled to think there were midshipmice training right now somewhere in the rambling stone building, his home. He tried to picture himself learning to be a warrior, and then he shook his head, twitching his round ears slightly. The idea was new and curious and too overwhelming to absorb.

Grandfather continued. "It is a hard yet gratifying life. Mice can't do everything humans can do." He let that thought settle for a minute, and then he added with a satisfied, whiskery grin, "But humans can't do everything *mice* can do."

"Hah, what's so hard about the things humans do?" Pip waved his paw with derision.

"Get up, Pip. Stand on your hind legs."

Pip rose from a squat and pulled his body straight up until he was supported entirely by his long, sharp-clawed back feet, balancing with his extended, sandpapery tail.

"Now what?" he asked with a furry, cheeky grin.

"Stay in that position until I tell you."

The others watched in silence while Pip stood erect on his hind legs. After a moment or two, his smile began to fade, his back hunched, and his hind quarters shook. He flopped back down with a wave of his front paw.

"This is stupid," he muttered and popped a crumb into his mouth.

Chester glanced sideways at Pip. What an embarrassing rodent. He admired the cool confidence of the midshipmice and Grandfather's calm assurance. That was the kind of mouse he wanted to be.

A new mouse, Dilly, whose family had just arrived in a packing crate from the West Coast, stood and courageously inquired from the back of the group, "What can we do to be selected? I wish to serve and protect."

"I admire your vigor, Dilly," Grandfather responded. "The elders have been watching, searching for those among you who stand out based on your honesty, willingness to help, and integrity."

More young mice turned away at these words, scuttling to beat each other to the warm spots near the silver heating columns that ran up the walls.

"We have been looking for those of you who exhibit physical ability and keenness of mind. We are looking for mice we can train into leaders. Do you think it is easy to leave your family and the horde for the duration of training and service? You must be willing to sacrifice everything for what is right."

Chester noticed one pompous fellow puffing out his fluffy chest, but most were wiggling uncomfortably, glancing at each other with round, wide eyes, twisting around to gnaw at itchy spots on their hind ends. Chester sat quietly, forelegs folded. The story was one he had heard before, but this time his whole being responded with excitement.

A squeaky voice whispered, "I'd rather nap when I want to and rummage about for food."

Chester thought the life of a household mouse sounded flat and boring compared to Grandfather's story describing the duties of a midshipmouse.

Grandfather stood and surveyed the furry group huddled at his feet. "The next class of midshipmouse candidates will be announced when the ground thaws and the pipes through the walls no longer send out their heat."

The old mouse ambled back to his nest to remove his uniform, leaving the young mice to wander off as they pleased. The new mouse, Dilly, remained, nodding to Chester as he passed.

Chester mulled over the grand size of the stone building in which he lived. He had never been allowed to investigate further than the few storerooms of food close to their household. He began to hum a melody and then sing the words of his favorite song:

> *Strings and strands and rubber bands,*
> *Pick up bits, make no plans.*
> *I won't hurry or wander far,*
> *Strings and strands and rubber bands.*

Chester sang off tune as he gathered some pebbles. He and his best friend, Theo, had been using them as projectiles for a catapult they had built with a small piece of wood and a wedge. They had spent hours shooting the stones through the air, watching them soar through the rafters to various target spots, until Mama had caught them and made them stop, saying they would put some mouse's eye out. Chester paused from collecting the small rocks. Who would be chosen? Was *he* qualified?

Chester moved purposefully to his comfy nest lined with fluff, gnawed paper, and soft material. His special belongings were stacked here and there in a semblance of order: braided rope in different sizes, small wires he had been examining, folded pages of writing, a chunk of glass that caught the light, a few nuts and crumbles tucked away for a hungry moment, and catapults of different sizes. He found his safety pin and set it out and then curled up to think. The image of the five midshipmice—confident, cool, and in charge—played in his head. He put his paws behind his ears and pictured all the possibilities for his future and tossed them out one by one.

*I did not run away from danger,* he thought. He now knew in his heart what he wanted more than anything. *I want to become a naval midshipmouse.*

Below the mouse household, in room 5016, human voices were heard through the ceiling boards on which the mice slept. The mice did not catch the words, only the muffled roar that echoed in the rafters as one midshipman shouted to his two roommates.

"Those mice got in my closet *again*. How do they get in here?"

"I think they have been here since Mother B was built. You would think after three years of living here, you would catch on by now. *Keep your food in plastic bins!*" his roommate replied in a mock weary tone.

"Yeah, well, maybe I'm a slow learner. I got another year to figure it out," the victim of the mice answered, cleaning crumbs out of his closet.

Their third roommate, a wiry, blond fellow, interrupted them. "I thought I smelled smoke for just a minute last night, then it went away. Anyone else notice that?"

"Must have been a dream," the annoyed midshipman replied, continuing to meticulously sweep up the crumbs, his hazel eyes narrowed in disgust. "Though I did hear a herd of little feet scampering in the ceiling."

"Good thing you didn't really smell smoke," the tallest of the three replied, pushing the trimmed auburn hair on his forehead up into a wave. "Last thing we need is the fire alarm going off in the middle of the night and having to stand in formation outside in the cold."

"Phew! Got that right."

## CHAPTER 2

# The Quest Begins

✠

CHESTER FOLDED THE OLD, WORN-OUT naval manuals lent to him by Grandfather Nimitz and made a decision: he would need to push himself out of his comfort zone. With a nod of his furry golden-brown snout, he confirmed the thought: he was going to have to take his physical training outside the walls of Bancroft Hall… where he rarely ventured.

After Grandfather's talk and the visit of the midshipmice, Chester had deposited his application into the box specifically marked for those who wanted to apply to the Naval Mouse Academy. The old blue matchbox with a large gold *N* painted in the center had already been stuffed with papers when he slipped his in.

Then he began to eat, sleep, and breathe his plans to become the best candidate possible. In the last twenty cycles of the moon, Chester had transformed himself from a quiet, steady young mouse into a studying, healthy-eating exercise machine, though he still ate chocolate cereal crisps for breakfast.

Poring over the USNMA manuals, he memorized the bewildering amount of technical terms, methodically plotted and planned.

"What do those initials mean?" his little brother Bean asked.

"United States Naval Mouse Academy," Chester replied abstractedly, his tawny nose following the words on the page. "Look,

Bean…look at the pictures of these exercises. If I'm accepted, I've got to be able to do more than fifty push-ups and fifty pull-ups and run fast and far the minute I show up on Induction Night."

"Induction Night?"

"Yes, that's the first night of training for every mouse given a letter of acceptance. It's a grueling introduction to the Naval Mouse Academy. It's supposed to be really stressful and feel never ending."

Bean's large, protruding eyes grew even wider in awe at the list of challenges Chester was describing. Chester took a deep breath of happy anticipation.

"You *want* to do this?" Bean asked, but Chester didn't even hear him.

Grandfather had taken Chester to see an old friend, Admiral Bilge (retired), who was an advisor for the Naval Mouse Academy and whose word carried heavy weight.

Admiral Bilge was a big, barrel-chested mouse with gray grizzled fur cut short between his knobby ears, slightly round in the belly, but otherwise still packing some muscle. He held himself erect during most of the interview, looking down his pointy nose at Chester. His questions were blunt and direct.

"Why do you think you should be selected? What are your strengths and weaknesses?"

Chester was prepared for many questions but not this one. He swallowed. How could he say he knew he was smart? That would be bragging. And how would he say that he knew he had not reached the acceptable level of strength and speed yet without sounding as though he was lacking?

"I'm a quick learner. I work hard and don't give up. I believe there are some who should protect the horde. I believe I'm one of them." He hoped the admiral would hear the sincere confidence in his voice.

"What is it that *you* want out of the experience, Chester?"

Chester thought briefly and then spoke quietly. "I admire my grandfather and want to be like him. I want to serve. I believe this is my future…and one day I want to fly in the sky."

Chester had never told anyone that he wished to ride in an airplane one day.

Admiral Bilge looked at him appraisingly. "Some mice have gone on to aviation but very few. We're mostly land and sea based. What if you never fly…would you still want to serve?"

Chester did not hesitate for a minute. "Absolutely…yes, sir," he added belatedly.

"We've had our eye on you, Chester. We only take the best and the brightest. Keep on learning, continue to train hard, and *stay out of trouble.* You're at the top of the list of household mouse applicants. Don't do *anything* to jeopardize your chances. Many mice are competing for a limited number of spots."

The words of encouragement thrilled Chester. He immediately spoke to his buddy Theo. They did everything together.

"Are you going to apply? We would make a great team—we could train together!"

Theo shook his head. "Nope, I'm meant to do something else, probably something to do with wires. I'm exploring which ones to chew, which ones not to, and how to twist them back together."

"What about all our catapults and working on our firing distances? You were always eager to do that."

"I loved building them and seeing what they could do, but I don't want to shoot at any living creatures. Chester, I'm backing you all the way, but this is not for me."

The two friends shook paws.

After the meeting with Admiral Bilge, Chester took his training regimen to the next level. He began to wave away cracker bits and cookie crumbs.

"Not enough oomph…no substance."

He ate pawfuls of dry oats for stamina, cheese shreds and nuts to keep up his strength, and the occasional raisin because he had a sweet tooth. Mama did her best to scavenge for nutritious snacks and was amazed at his unwavering determination.

Next, he decided he needed to train exactly like the midshipmice he had read about in Grandfather's manuals. He would need to venture outside of Bancroft Hall to challenge himself in long-distance scampering.

For several nights he slipped out well before dawn, the time he normally went to sleep. Mama and Papa were now accustomed to him charging along beams and shimmying up pipes throughout the rafters of their rambling household to perform his nightly exercise, so they didn't notice his absence. By leaving a series of knotted strings and navigating a maze of protruding rough gray-and-beige stones on the outside of Bancroft Hall, Chester made a path to the outside world. He told Bean but cautioned him not to tell Mama and Papa.

"They would worry too much. If I'm going to be a midshipmouse, I am going to have to make important decisions on my own."

The freedom was exhilarating. At first he had run tentatively, watching out for owls and voles and staying close to the foundation of the building. The lights surrounding the vast structure cast his shadow, triangle body with head low to the ground. He glanced at the wall to see the dark reflection of his round belly and hindquarters, his long, slender tail whipping along behind. He knew how much time he had and listened for the clock in the tower to chime. The nights were chilly; puffs of steam bellowed out of his nostrils as he chugged along.

On the third night, he ventured a little further away from the large stone walls, crossed a courtyard, and scurried down a brick usan Weisberg

path. He was shocked when he came across a group of mice wearing white T-shirts with blue trim around the collar tucked into blue short pants, running and calling out to each other as they pounded down the path at a good clip.

"Faster! Gotta be able to do this in under seven minutes!"

"Piece of cheese."

"Yah? Wait until the physical-fitness test next week. You'll be blubbering because you ate too much cheese."

"I've passed every PFT so far. I got this."

"You got *fleas*!"

They all laughed.

Midshipmice!

Chester shrank into the crisp grass alongside the red bricks, but they barely glanced at him. He knew they had seen him and assessed his presence, but they passed with the briefest of nods.

Chester redoubled his efforts.

"Only the best, only the best," he chanted in his head, remembering Admiral Bilge's words as he ran harder and faster until he felt a little stitch in his left haunch. He circled back and headed for the ladder of stones and the hidden crevice into Bancroft Hall while the dark sky still sparkled with stars.

The next night Papa noticed Chester's slight limp and asked the reason.

"Probably pulled a muscle."

"Put a cold stone on it," Papa advised. "Give it a rest."

But Chester was not about to quit training. Maybe it was only a charley horse from all the running. He was on a mission to be in the finest shape possible and couldn't waste a minute. He continued to push himself, hammering along the hard paths of the Yard where the naval mice trained by night and humans trained by day.

In the wee hours, just when the midshipmen below were turning over in their sleep and longing for a few more hours of rest, Chester snuck out of the household mouse living area.

He began this night's run in a different direction from before—alongside a jutting wing of the building, down a ramp and some steps, and across an expanse of asphalt painted with lines. Except for the lingering ache in his haunch, he felt fine.

*I'll shake it off,* he thought and pushed himself to run further than before.

The nagging stab in his thigh continued. Just as he found himself along a low sea wall, the pain became worse, and he was forced to stop and rest. He stooped, whiskers drooping and chest heaving, and rubbed his hind leg. Chester was in trouble. The ache was now deep and throbbing. He was a long way from home and still had to get back.

On the other side of the low cement barrier, he thought he heard a little splashing. Was it a midshipmouse boat? How he longed to see the mice sailing their naval vessels. He found some chinks in the wall and pulled himself up by his front paws and one hind leg until he stood upon a flat surface. Peering over the edge, he squinted through the dark toward the lapping water that reflected the light of the streetlamps overhead. At first he saw nothing. Then a snout with a thick sprout of whiskers appeared, followed by a smooth head with short, slippery fur. The creature spied Chester, bared its teeth, and lunged forward. A water rat! He backed up abruptly. Which way should he scamper along the wall? In the split second before he made his decision, paws grabbed him from behind, and a voice spoke urgently into his ear.

"Jump!"

He felt himself sailing backward onto the pavement below.

He landed in a furry heap on top of four mice dressed in bluish-toned camouflage clothing, who had braced his fall. The two identically dressed mice who had appeared behind him on the seawall landed alongside. The group dragged Chester between them away from the water's edge. No one spoke until they had crossed a road and reached the shelter of a bush.

"You idiot! What the hilly-hooey do you think you are doing? Trying to get yourself and everyone else killed!"

Chester looked at the cloth tape stitched with a name—Spleen—sewn in capital letters over the breast pocket of the angry mouse who reared on his hind legs, glaring into his face. The other mice all had their names on their uniforms as well.

"Water rat..." Chester uttered.

His mind was whirling. This was the waterfront patrol—the midshipmice charged with guarding against the water rat. He had made a major blunder.

"Yes, a river otter. Didn't you know that this area is off-limits to mice?"

"Back off, Spleen," the voice of a female mouse spoke more civilly. "He probably didn't know. Look, rodent, what's your name?"

"Chester," he answered quietly.

He wished he could make up a different name, but he had to tell the truth. Lying was a terrible offense in the Naval Mouse Academy. It was a matter of honor. He had always been an honest mouse, anyway.

"All right, we're going to escort you out of this area or to the gates of the Yard. Town mouse, house mouse, or field mouse?"

Chester told them that he was a house mouse of Bancroft Hall.

He limped home, slinking on all fours between the midshipmice, who had stones in their paws at the ready for protection. Pain shot through his leg with every step. The midshipmice escorted him to the entrance to his household, where Mama and Papa—who had started to wonder where he was—greeted him with alarm showing on their faces. Grandfather perched right behind them, rubbing his eyes sleepily. They were astonished to see him in the company of six midshipmice wearing camouflage jackets. He was in deep trouble in so many ways. Chester faced his family with his painful hind leg lifted off the floor.

Grandfather assessed the situation.

"Well, let's see. You didn't tell anyone where you were going and ventured into an area that was off-limits, putting yourself and others in danger."

"Yes, though I didn't know I was in the restricted area."

"And now your name has been placed in an official report that will show up on your application."

"Yes, but I didn't tell a lie."

"*And* you have an injured leg that you can't run on."

Chester miserably pressed his lips together over his long front teeth. "Yes."

"Well, it's not the best timing," Grandfather said in a massive understatement. "What do you want to do?"

*Vomit*, Chester thought, but he quickly pulled himself together. "I'll do anything. What can I do?"

Mama muttered, wringing her paws, "There's a way out of this…I know there is! Oh, poor Chester!"

Grandfather spoke to Papa, who had been standing quietly the whole time.

"What do you think is wrong with his leg? Is it the bone in his haunch?"

Papa spoke seriously from behind his glasses, his bullnose snout wrinkled in thought as he pressed on the sore area of Chester's leg.

"I think it may be only a stressful ping or twang to the bone, because he can bear weight, but it's a matter of concern. He certainly cannot run or even walk long distances," he remarked as Chester grimaced with pain.

Grandfather watched Papa examine Chester's haunch, pushing on the muscle of his round hip and flexing the joint. Grandfather bluntly announced the hard reality of the situation.

"Even if Chester is selected, he will not make it through the admission process on Induction Night if he is not completely healed. No mouse is accepted to the Naval Mouse Academy with any sort of debilitating injury. They will reject him and send him home if he does not walk through the entrance hole totally healthy. *And* he will never pass the physical requirement test."

Chester felt tears pricking behind his eyes and blinked rapidly so that no one would see. He was so close! How could this be happening?

"If he stays off the leg, he will lose all the benefits of his training, but that may be our only choice."

Chester realized gratefully that Grandfather, Papa, and Mama were on his side. They *wanted* him to succeed. He glanced at Grandfather, trying to see if he was angry or disappointed in him. He didn't know if he was more upset with himself for ruining his own chances for admission or letting Grandfather down.

"There's another option. I have an idea," Papa interrupted. "We can change the method of Chester's exercise and see if he can heal while still building strength. It's worth a try."

Grandfather arched a graying brow in question. "I'm all ears," he commented. "What is this miracle exercise?"

"He will need to exercise without putting any weight on his hind leg. He will need to learn how to swim."

Chester was willing to do anything. He would swim an ocean if he had to. He was positive he could do it if he was given enough practice. There was only one problem.

"But how, Papa? We're not allowed at the waterfront."

"Leave that to me."

Two nights later Papa led them through a gap in the ceiling to the floor below and then behind several walls until they squeezed into a small room containing a human sink and a toilet. They all slid down gleaming white porcelain until they were gathered on a ring of white plastic suspended over water. Papa took the strong rope he had been carrying and wrapped it around Chester's chest, knotting it securely. The other end he attached to a pipe running up the wall.

Chester peered down into the calm, clear water of the toilet bowl and swallowed. It looked awfully deep. He tugged at the square knot at his furry chest and glanced at the other end of the rope triple wrapped around the pipe. Was he going to be able to stay afloat?

"Are you ready, Chester?" Papa asked in a bracing tone.

Chester thought about all the hours he had spent running, building up muscle and stamina, scurrying and scuttling in the chill of the night. He clenched his jaw and sucked in his lip over his prominent front teeth. He was not going to let his hard work go down the drain. He took a deep breath.

Papa and Grandfather perched on the rim of the toilet seat and watched as Chester jumped in. They called instructions to stay afloat, to use his forelegs, kick with his back unless it hurt the injured leg, and whip with his tail. Papa held on to the rope. Circling the edge of the bowl, Chester swam awkwardly and then with more success until he was out of breath. He pulled himself out by the safety line, water matting his fur and dripping off his tail, exhausted but encouraged.

This method worked so well that within a week he declared he needed more of a challenge. Theo, who had come along to watch and cheer him on, had an idea. He brought a thick rubber band along with Bean, Allie-Poo, and a few more of Chester's siblings to the bathroom. He threw the circlet of rubber over a handle on the side of the gleaming white ceramic tank. Papa and Grandfather shortened the rope tethered to Chester until it held him just at the surface of the water.

"Hang on!" they shouted.

Theo, Bean, Allie-Poo, and the others jumped up, grabbed hold, and swung on the dangling end of the rubber band until their weight caused the toilet to flush. Chester was supposed to swim against the current until the water disappeared and refilled again. The first flush was such a shock that Chester twirled wildly round and round before being left hanging in midair.

Bean was shouting, "Woo-hoo!"

Allie-Poo had her paws over her eyes, sure that Chester would be sucked into the pipes.

"Centrifuge," Chester announced weakly once he stopped whirling, a little green around the snout.

The next flush produced better results, as Chester was able to swim a few strokes before getting swept along in the vortex. Night after night, flush after flush, he swam until his body became stronger and stronger.

With a worried frown, Papa pressed on Chester's sore leg and commented hopefully that maybe he might be able to overcome his injury after all. Grandfather checked the calendar, counting off the nights until the acceptances would be announced and then counting again the sunsets and moonrises until Induction Night. It was tight. Would he even be accepted?

Chester replayed the scene of being rescued by the midship-mice over and over in his head. The words of Admiral Bilge echoed in his mind: "Stay out of trouble." Chester clutched his stomach.

❦

Below the mouse household, in room 5016, one of the human midshipmen awakened and jumped out of his rack, stepping down from his neatly made bed to his desk and then to the floor. He always slept on top of his blanket so he would not have to remake his bed with painstaking precision every morning, wasting valu-able time. He reached up and gave the sheet a tweak.

"Hey, man, did you hear that toilet flushing all night? What's up with that?"

"Beats me. Must be out of order, or someone wasn't feeling too well."

"Can't be the food. The meals in King Hall are pretty decent. How soon till breakfast?"

"Thirty minutes. Better not be the stomach bug going around. I can't afford to catch it."

"Well, whatever it is, I hope they fix it soon. I need my sleep. Though with finals coming up, I'll probably be up all night anyway."

CHAPTER 3

# The Journey Begins

❧

CHESTER SHIVERED IN THE TWILIGHT hour. The day had been long and hot, but right now it was almost completely dark, and the air was cool in the shadows of a large stone building across the Yard from Bancroft Hall. It was not the usual time for him to be up and out of his nest, but Mama had come fussing at him while the sun was still up, licking her paws and smoothing the fur between his ears, trying to make it lie flat. She had brought him a corner of wheat toast and a chunk of cheese, but he was too excited to eat. During his sleep he thought he had heard the sound of jets screaming overhead.

*Induction Day for the humans,* he had thought sleepily, restless in the stirred-up material of his nest.

Now it was Induction Night for the mice, or INight, as Grandfather called it, and Chester was lining up with the other candidates.

He peered through the dark to see the other mice joining him in line and thought about what Grandfather had said about the opposite training schedules kept by the mice and the humans.

The advantage to being nocturnal, Grandfather had told him, was that the mice and humans rarely interacted with each other.

"We know our place. We are not to interfere. Neither are they to interfere with us. Together we train new officers and work to protect the building and naval yard night and day. We can borrow provisions freely during the night, and the humans go about their business during the day while we sleep. Precise military planning."

*Suppose it keeps us from accidently being stepped on,* Chester thought.

Chester shivered again when he thought how close he had come to being rejected by the Naval Mouse Academy. Just when his hind haunch had calmed to a dull ache, and he had started to feel hopeful again about possible acceptance to the Naval Mouse Academy, Admiral Bilge had paid Grandfather a visit. Chester had been summoned to be a part of the confidential discussion. Admiral Bilge had divulged that the admission committee was meeting again to discuss his application. They were now concerned with his reliability.

Admiral Bilge had dropped the words like bombs.

"Your name was so high on the admission list that the committee was ready to offer you an early acceptance. Now they are reconsidering that offer. In fact, any offer."

Chester was so shocked that he had trouble catching his breath.

"What did the committee members say?" Grandfather asked quietly.

"Some thought he was a loose cannon once they learned he had been found in the restricted area and had to be rescued from the water rat."

"Anything else? I know you are sharing this information as a favor. Tell us the worst, we'd better hear it all." Grandfather's voice was grim.

"'Not sure he's the right material,' one of the old rodents commented." Admiral Bilge turned to Chester, speaking sternly. "But

I rooted for you. Pointed out your fine qualities and positive attri-
butes. Did it out of respect for your grandfather."

"Yes, sir." Chester's tongue was as dry as cotton. "Thank you, sir."

"He's got the right stuff, Pump," Grandfather spoke strongly.

Chester was surprised to hear Grandfather use a nickname for
this imposing admiral mouse.

"Hope they can overlook the honest mistake he made. He had
no intention of disregarding rules."

Grandfather's support gave Chester a little lump in his throat.

"I understand that, Nim, but they may not." Admiral Bilge
turned to Chester. "I am only sharing this with you because I think
you should be prepared for disappointment. If they *do* decide to
give you an appointment, you are going to have to tread very carefully because the upper ranks will be watching you."

Chester had continued to swim furiously—anything to keep his
mind off waiting and wondering what would happen if the committee decided against him. He couldn't even think about that
possibility without getting dizzy.

After a month of leg rest except for swimming, his hind haunch
no longer ached. Chester had tested his recovery by running on
the soft, pink insulation material lining the beams in the upper
rafters to avoid jarring the healing injury. He was pleased to discover that he could jog along without pain while on the soft surface. On Papa's advice he did not push running any harder. He
continued swimming, amazed at the endurance he achieved, and
anxiously waited for an answer.

One night, when the air outside had turned soft with the first
whisper of a warm breeze, the official paper had been nailed up
on a beam at the entrance to the mouse household with the names
of those mice living in the walls and ceilings of Bancroft Hall who

had been chosen. Nervously, Chester scanned the list, fear sitting like a rock in the pit of his stomach. He did not see his name until the very bottom. With relief he read, "Chester."

A normally quiet and contained mouse, he shouted with joy and amused his siblings by running in circles, dancing on his hind legs, and thrusting his forepaws into the air in triumph. Theo clapped his furry back over and over.

Now in the still, cool of INight, Chester was determined to show he was ready and capable. He looked around in surprise at the streams of mice arriving from the fields and faraway cities. They nodded to each other nonchalantly as each joined up in line. Some rodents had even traveled by ship from other countries, catching a ride in the cargo. All were reporting at the same time, anxious to start their training to become an officer, ready to be sworn in to the United States Naval Mouse Academy. Chester felt prepared for the grueling challenge and looked forward to the reward, which would be to earn the right to serve as a naval mouse officer. Plebe Summer was about to begin.

Dilly had also been chosen and stood behind him in the growing line of teeny creatures stretched along the foundation of Alumni Hall, the admission center. Some tried to look relaxed, while others nervously flicked their tails and shifted from one paw to another, glancing around to peer at their fellow classmates out of the corner of their bulging eyes and sizing each other up. No one spoke. As the clock in the tower ticked the minutes by, more and more mice appeared, holding only a few necessities in their paws: a fur brush, dental floss, whisker trimmers. One had a pistachio nut, which was quickly confiscated. Only personal grooming items and a form of identification were allowed.

Chester pulled a rolled postage stamp out of the little bag held tightly in his paw. It had been etched with his name at birth and signed by an elder of their household. Last night Mama had taken him to her soft nest and riffled through a very tall stack of stamps tucked in the corner, all bearing the name of one of her babies. The tower of official papers was held in place against any breezes by a copper penny.

"Let's see..." She began peering at each one, reading aloud the names of his many brothers and sisters.

"Allie-Poo, wrong litter...Beanie Boy...Forever...*Forever?* Oh, wait, that's a blank one. Here you are—*Chester!*" She handed him the stamp with the picture of a red, white, and blue flag.

"Don't lose this," she had warned, her eyes welling up with tears. "It's the only record of your birth." Mama had searched his furry face as if to memorize it and gave a brave, watery smile. "We'll miss you, but I know you'll do well."

Slowly the mice inched forward until they moved through a gap in the stone and were led to rows of tables. Chester was going to have to be sharp and on his game. He held his postage stamp in his paw. Some mice had small pinecone kernels inscribed with their names clasped in their claws. *Field mice*, he thought.

"Name!" barked a midshipmouse with the insignia of a first-class, or senior, student.

"Chester," he replied firmly.

"What?" the upperclassmouse roared in response.

"Chester, sir!" Chester tried again.

Now two menacing, towering mice stood over him, their whiskers tickling his face.

"From now on, when you answer any question, you start with 'sir' and end with 'sir.' And *don't* look at me. Name."

Chester gulped and stared straight ahead. "Sir, Chester, sir!" Chester blurted out what would be the first of many sir sandwiches shouted that summer.

He was given a large white duffel bag filled with new belongings and told to change quickly. The bag contained a loose white canvas shirt, which they called a blouse; a belt with a shiny buckle; baggy white pants; and a cup-shaped hat with a dark-blue stripe around the rim. As rapidly as he could, hurried along by threatening shouts and commands, he dressed in the awkward, unfamiliar clothes. Standing as instructed, with his hind toes forty-five degrees apart and his paws curled, yet rigid along the side seams of his shirt, Chester found he was holding his breath as an upperclassmouse bellowed.

"You are now in a uniform. This is the cloth of our nation. You will wear it with pride and respect it!"

Chester's heart thrilled at the words while he scurried to follow commands and avoid the wrath of the shouting mice. He joined line after line of mice in the basement of the building. In one corner designated Health Section, a graying mouse pressed on his round tummy and peered seriously into his mouth and pink ears using a gigantic magnifying glass. With a paw held over a clipboard, he went over Chester's health history.

"Any injuries?"

Chester's breath caught in his throat. Seconds ticked by as he thought what to say. He would have to be honest.

"Sir, I did have a slight ping to my left rear haunch. It is completely healed now, sir!"

Chester hoped he was healed. He waited in suspense. Would the Health Department mouse believe him or ask him to leave? The old mouse lowered his snout and looked intently at Chester. He leaned around to peer and probe at the mentioned leg. Then he took his writing implement and made a check mark somewhere on the page.

"Move on." He waved Chester through.

Chester exhaled in relief. But what did the mark on his record mean?

At another station the fur on his head was trimmed down to almost nothing. He realized that he now was standing among a throng of mice he did not know. They were handed small blue books and told to start memorizing the words as they stood at attention, forelegs bent, books held directly in front of their pale noses, eyes glued to the pages.

When they were to put the little blue books away, the trainers shouted in loud voices, "Stow your trash!"

The anxious mice whipped their books in and out of their pockets trying to keep up with the commands of their detailers, the upperclassmice assigned to train them for the summer.

Some of the mice needed glasses and were given big, thick lenses with black rims and ear straps, which were pretty funny looking. Except for the color of their fur, the mice looked identical.

At one table, they were informed of their company numbers. This assignment would determine the group of mice they would live with, eat with, and learn with for the next four seasons. Each company had a separate sleeping space in Bancroft Hall. Thirty companies comprised the Brigade of Midshipmice, and over the years, each one had developed its own reputation and way of doing things. Some were said to be lenient, while others were known to be far more rigid with keeping all the rules. During Plebe Summer there would be forty to fifty plebe mice per company. In the academic year, the number in each company would swell to more than a hundred when the older midshipmice came back from summer assignments to resume their studies.

Chester shuffled forward right behind the mouse in front of him, eyes locked on the shiny gray fur showing above the mouse's collar, trying to remember to do everything right. He was anxious to discover which company would become his new "family." Ever since he had received his appointment to the Naval Mouse Academy, Chester had been hoping he would like his shipmates, as members of the company were called, and hoped they would like and respect him too. He had been excited to report for Induction Night, but now as the night unfolded, his stomach was full of butterflies. He wanted to make his grandfather proud, and he also wanted to make himself proud.

Inching forward, eyes straight ahead, Chester stood in front of the elderly mouse, who pawed through the file box of papers, muttering names aloud.

"Cadence...Calvin...Cecil...Chambers...Clover..." The grizzled mouse looked down his long nose while separating papers with his claws. "Um...wait a second, went too far. Let me back up...Chester." He whipped out the official note and handed it to Chester: Sixth Company.

The same company as Grandfather! The tradition of naval service begun with his grandfather would continue with Chester. His heart swelled. He looked more closely at the thick square of paper. The words *Fifth Company* had been crossed out and *Sixth Company* written underneath in bold lettering. Grandfather had told him that in his day Fifth Company had been known for its by-the-book leadership. They followed every rule to the letter. No wiggle room. He wiggled just thinking about his close escape. Why had they switched his company assignment?

*Missed that one by the skin of my teeth*, he thought.

Chester and a few others were herded into an alcove and stood, silent and nervous, until more young mice were grouped together into the smaller unit, or squad. While they waited, a tall midshipmouse in a spotless white uniform with black shoulder boards taught them, in a very loud voice, how to hold their paws at an angle in a proper salute. They were learning very quickly to avoid making mistakes. A mistake was costly. It drew unwanted attention and consequences for the mouse who made an error and often for his or her shipmates too. Chester soon found himself on the ground doing push-ups, keeping his tense, dry nose pointed forward so it wouldn't scrape the ground, all because another mouse forgot to say sir.

"Plebes! What's up!" their detailer roared.

The mice stood silent, confused. The detailer answered his own question.

"The only proper response is 'fidelity is up, and obedience is down on our bayonet buckles!'"

The new plebe mice shouted, "Sir! Fidelity is up, and obedience is down on our bayonet buckles, sir!"

"Why do we say that?" a large, blotchy brown plebe mouse whispered.

"*Fidelity* and *obedience* are engraved on the top and bottom of the human's belt buckles," another new fellow plebe mouse with white fur hissed back in a tone that implied that every mouse knew that.

"You have something you want to share?" the detailer in the spotless white uniform barked.

"Sir, no, sir!" the two plebe mice shouted, while the others inwardly cringed with dismay.

Juggling their blue books, new hats, and canteens, they were brusquely told to toss their heavy bags onto a skateboard that had just been rolled up to carry their gear. Chester and the other young rodents—or plebes, as they were now being called in loud voices—trotted along behind as the skateboard made its way through night-shadowed alleyways until they were back at Bancroft Hall. Their bulging bags of issued clothing and equipment were pitched onto the ground by enlisted rodents, while glaring upper-classmice, whiskers twitching, barked at them to find their gear and form up into lines. The young plebe mice scrambled to find places in line, dropping their bags and fumbling with their strange sailor caps that tipped down on their long cone-shaped sweaty foreheads.

Chester kept trying to push it back up to the proper distance from his eyes, using two claws of his paw to measure the space between his eye whiskers and the rim of the cap. As he stood at attention, Chester spied Dilly at the end of his row, chin tucked, face rigid. Dilly was in Sixth Company too. He felt a small sense of relief among the growing pressure.

Chester was concentrating so hard on hearing directions and following them that he did not see the large group of rodent families and friends who had gathered to catch a glimpse of the new plebes. Tears and shouts of encouragement rang out from the growing crowd of relatives. Chester's parents stood among the horde, perched on a curb, nervous to be outside the protection of Bancroft Hall. They were searching for his familiar furry snout as cart after cart rolled in under the streetlights. The plebe mice all looked so much alike that it was hard to find him.

"There he is!" Mama cried.

"No, there he is!" Papa pointed, craning his snout to see over the ears of other mice.

They were never quite sure if they saw him among the sea of white uniforms continuously forming and reforming under the large stone steps.

Before they could catch their breath, the plebe mice were marched inside in untidy rows, trying to keep in step with those around them and out the way of the intimidating, shouting detailers whose attention was to be avoided at all costs.

Chester's round cap slipped and tilted as he shifted and flicked his ears, struggling to keep it in place. He discovered that the stubbly bits of fur on the top of his newly shorn head helped hold it in place. His new haircut felt funny, but if this was what it took to become a midshipmouse, he was all for it. They were led in their new squads at full scurry up the pipes to the unfamiliar area where they would now be living. In the dim light, Chester saw row after row of square nests neatly lining the floor, each one separated by a wall of woven twigs and thatch. Everything was immaculate and clean, not a crumb or strand out of place. His assigned detailer, Mr. Bravo, paused between each of their new nests, now called quarters, and shouted the names of the plebe mice who would be sleeping there.

"Chester. Dilly. Ranger."

Chester could not believe his good fortune. Dilly was not only in his company but was also his nestmate. They tumbled through the entrance and turned to greet the stranger occupying a corner of their shiny floored quarters right next to a matt of fluff that he had already claimed as his bed. Standing up from where he crouched to sort his neatly stacked belongings, the very large mouse with an auburn pelt and chunky, pearly white teeth extended a massive paw.

"Hi, my name's Ranger." He grinned.

There was no time for hellos. Chester and Dilly managed a paw clasp and quickly dropped their bags before they were off and running to line up against the wall outside the nests.

"Let the bellowing begin," Ranger muttered out of the corner of his mouth with a cocky grin. Clearly he was not intimidated by the yelled verbal volleys happening all around them.

"Plebe mice! This is called the bulkhead, just like on a ship. You do not call it a wall!" shouted one of the detailers as he strolled by on all fours.

Chester perched on his hind legs at attention, shoulders back and squared, chin tucked, staring straight ahead, blue book held directly in front of his nose, hoping he would not draw attention by making a mistake. He had learned already that he should not stand out in *any* way. And he especially did not want to be recognized as the mouse who had entered into the restricted area and had to be rescued.

"Watch your bearing."

A passing detailer stopped in front of Ranger and pushed his whiskered nose in so close that all Chester could see out of the corner of his eye was a glimpse of a yellow shirt, which most of the detailers were wearing.

"What's so *funny*?" he roared into Ranger's snout.

Chester did not look but could hear Ranger's firm reply.

"Sir, I'll find out and report back, sir."

The mouse miraculously moved on, and Chester snuck a peek at Ranger, who gave him a wink. Chester was sweating under his fur, but Ranger looked cool as a cucumber.

Chester and Dilly later found out that Ranger was prior enlisted. A few young rodents who had served as enlisted mice in various places were sent to the Naval Mouse Academy as potential officer material. Ranger had already been on gigantic navy ships and even flown in planes. In the spring, he had marched off the gangplank of his latest assigned ship, with a green sea bag over his broad shoulder and the acceptance letter in his paw, and traveled for weeks, hopping on any vehicle going in the right direction, finally arriving in the side bag of a motorcycle at the gates of the Naval Mouse Academy. He knew the ropes.

Later that first night when they were back in their quarters, Ranger rapidly showed Chester and Dilly how to neatly roll and stow their new, unfamiliar clothes to maximize space. He demonstrated how to smooth the wrinkles out of their uniforms by blowing hot breath onto their paws, rubbing them together briskly, and smoothing them over the stiff white material. Chester soon realized that Ranger's inside military knowledge was a valuable bonus and mentally shook his snout at his good fortune. He was quickly readjusting his thoughts on how to survive and thrive in this new environment. Having Ranger as a nestmate was a definite advantage to avoid costly mistakes. He was grateful they had been assigned together.

Chester was still lined up with the others on the bulkhead when a flash of yellow stopped directly in front of him.

"Plebe mouse, what's your name?"

"Sir, Chester, sir!" He knew this response by heart now.

"Oh, Mr. Chester. Heard about *you*. We keep our eye on mice like you."

The detailer moved on.

Ranger whispered, "Ignore him. They say stuff like that to rattle you."

But Chester feared that the detailer really had heard about him. Admiral Bilge had warned him he would be watched.

The running, yelling, shouting, and snapping to attention continued for the rest of Induction Night. Every time the plebes stopped, they pulled out their little blue books, held them straight out in front of their bulging eyes, and shouted the words that would soon become routine.

"To develop midshipmice morally, mentally, and physically and to imbue them with the highest ideals of duty, honor, and loyalty… sir!"

When every mouse had been processed, examined, instructed, and grouped into companies, and then into smaller squads, they

were marched into the courtyard of Bancroft Hall, where all the mouse families had been invited to gather under the stars. It was one last chance for grandparents, mamas, papas, families, and friends to glimpse the new naval mouse students for a long, long time. The commandant of midshipmice, Captain Thunder, stood on the steps in front of the excited, cheering proud families, his furry chest clothed in white and covered in medals. He loudly administered the oath to the silent, subdued new plebe mice.

"Do you solemnly swear," he began as he named the responsibilities and duties of a United States Naval Mouse Academy midshipmouse.

"If so, say, 'I do.'"

The young mice, sailor caps in place, stretching as far as the eye could see, shouted in unison, "I do!"

"Nicely done!" Captain Thunder shouted back. "Welcome aboard, shipmates!"

The night wore on. The weary young mice, who were used to snacking every few hours while awake, were led for a second time to the clean, orderly tables of their dining hall. Chester remembered to tuck his cover under the bench. He did not want to make the mistake of putting it on the table, as another mouse had done. They ate sitting straight up, perched on the front quarter inch of the benches, eyes looking forward, not speaking unless they were spoken to.

Seated across from Chester was the stocky field mouse with blotchy fur. The name pin on his sailor blouse said Bodie. Bodie seemed more concerned with his food than his manners and subsequently spilled crumbs down the front of his white tunic. Chester was getting increasingly nervous for him, wishing he could warn him to brush away the hard corn chunks and flour bits, but he wasn't allowed to speak. Unable to look anywhere else, he watched the growing debris with alarm and diminishing appetite. A voice behind him bellowed. Chester was surprised to hear the harsh tones coming from a *female.*

"Mr. Bodie, where do you think you come from, *the farm?*"

"Ma'am, yes, ma'am," Bodie replied solidly, continuing to chew.

"You have the manners of a *pig.*"

"Ma'am, yes, ma'am…I mean…no, ma'am?" Bodie was confused.

Forgetting the rules he turned to look at his new squad mates for help. The mice continued to stare straight ahead in silence, paws held motionless in front of their chests, eating forgotten. The detailer with the strident voice sped around the table and reared up on her hind legs over the hapless mouse. Chester glanced quickly to see her name tag: Roxie.

"Eyes forward," Miss Roxie ranted at Bodie. "Eyes in the boat."

Sweat formed under Chester's collar. Some of the mice began to pant. The rest sat rigid, eyes fixed, not moving a whisker or twitching an ear. It was hot under the rafters of their dining hall, but they were sweating from fear. What would be the punishment for having bad manners? It seemed there were little punishments for everything.

"Your shipmates will be happy to help you. In fact, you all will clean up the floor after everyone has eaten."

Miss Roxie looked at Chester and read the name tag pinned to his loose white uniform top.

"Oh, you're the rodent who doesn't think the rules are for him."

She didn't wait for an answer, which was a good thing because Chester didn't have one. Nobody asked him later about the comment because they thought it was just the rough hazing they all were to expect.

Chester gritted his teeth. The detailers knew his name. He had a reputation before he even stepped through the entrance hole, and it wasn't a good one—all because he had unknowingly run into the restricted area where the water rat had been spotted.

Chester and his squad mates were held until the last squad left the dining hall, then they ran to wipe, sweep, scrub, and lick (in Bodie's case) the floor clean. Miss Roxie and other detailers stood over them hollering and urging them to work faster. Late to catch up with the rest of Sixth Company, the exhausted plebe mice had already forgotten much of what they had learned hours earlier. Tumbling at a near run, tails rigid, claws skittering across the floorboards, the nine errant plebe mice were rushed back to the wing of Bancroft Hall, where their company of forty-five new plebe mice had already gathered.

In the dark, in the winding, beamed spaces where plebe mice had been training for more than one hundred years, they could hear the melodic strains of singing. For as long as there had been midshipmice in Bancroft Hall, they had ended their nights by singing "Navy Blue and Gold." Tonight the singing was quiet because the plebe mice did not yet know the words or the tune.

*"Sea to sea...sailors brave in battle fair..."*

Chester stood against the bulkhead, blue book in front of his eyes, mumbling along with the song and hoping he could make it to lights-out without another violation.

Fifteen hours after passing through the entrance hole in the admission basement, getting their gear, learning to stand and salute, being screamed at, memorizing words, running and sweating, forgetting and answering incorrectly, being shown their new quarters, and getting in trouble at their second meal, Chester, Dilly, and Ranger were finally ordered to fall into their new quarters and go to sleep. No one needed to be told. The nestmates crawled into the unfamiliar, neatly arranged beds, or racks, as they were called, ready to drop.

It was awfully quiet. For a moment Chester wondered what had possessed him to want to do this. He ran his paw over the short prickly hairs between his ears. He could feel a warm draft on his scalp. The very first night of his life as a midshipmouse had not been heroic or exciting. It had been stressful, never ending, and humbling.

Silence held. Then in the dark, Dilly's voice spoke matter-of-factly. "Well, *this* was the longest night of my life."

There was a pause, and then the three burst out laughing together, Chester and Dilly muffling the low, squeaky chuckles with their paws. Chester smiled to himself and curled gingerly up in a ball in his corner, trying not to stir up the neat arrangement of straw and fluff. The challenges of the monumental day had been immense, but the moment of secret laughter had sparked a bond. The friendship of these two fellow mice was going to mean far more than he ever knew.

⚜

Under the nests where Chester, Dilly, and Ranger slept, below the ceiling tiles, in room 1324, eighteen-year-old Midshipman Fourth-Class B. Wise had just sprung out of his rack, as had his roommate T. Briggs. They were flying through the room in the predawn hour, throwing on shorts, T-shirts, long white socks, and new white sneakers, bumping into each other as they tried to be ready and out the door within the few minutes allotted.

"Are your folks sending you a package right away?" B. Wise asked fellow plebe, T. Briggs.

His new roommate was busy memorizing the food menu to be served that day in King Hall, where they ate three meals.

Remembering daily facts, known as chow call, had started right away.

Briggs recited out loud: "Orange juice, assorted cereal cups, country sausage gravy…yeah, my Mom sent one before I even got here, so it will be here soon. You know we need a flag displayed, even though we weren't allowed to bring one…Southern-style biscuit, scrambled egg with cheese. She said parents were told to package any snacks they send in plastic bins…country ham, fresh bagel, butter pat, fresh fruit. Apparently there can be a mouse problem here."

Both young men paused, looked around their neat and orderly room, shrugged, and then sprinted out the door as Briggs finished his litany of memorization for chow call.

"Assorted yogurt, milk, coffee…"

# CHAPTER 4

# The Long, Hot Summer

❖

CHESTER JUMPED OUT OF HIS rack as though he had been shot out of a cannon. The detailers banged on pipes and shouted into nests as they awakened the groggy plebe mice in their quarters up and down the passageway. Claws scraped and tails slapped as the startled mice hit the ground running.

He tried to yank his blue shorts up over his tail while hopping on one foot to examine a sore on his heel and gingerly check out the chafed areas on his hind legs where his white works were beginning to rub off fur.

*Think of it as a game,* he reminded himself, as he did every night when he first woke up.

Chester, Dilly, and Ranger raced to smooth out the blue blankets on top of their compact nests of fluff with quick swipes of their paws. It was easier to sleep on top of the blankets in order to save time when straightening their racks. Besides, it was too hot to sleep under a piece of cloth anyway.

The detailers herded them with barked orders as they joined the other mice of Sixth Company scurrying along the dark inside passages, shimmying down metal pipes, one after another, to exit Bancroft Hall. They were urged to move with haste to the large field outside, their acorn water canteens sloshing with each quick step.

After three nights the other new plebe mice were beginning to become familiar to Chester, especially the eight other mice in his squad: Dilly, Ranger, Brown Bob—a short, tough mouse with a glossy brown coat—Bodie, Ella—a small, confident harvest mouse—JP, Fleet, and Victor—an exchange mouse from Europe.

The mice of Sixth Company were joined on the drill field by the rodents of Fifth Company for evening PEP, the rigorous exercises they performed as soon as they were awakened and rushed outside into the warm night.

A muscular detailer, his yellow shirt reflecting the light of the overhead lamps, stood on an overturned bucket and bellowed into a piece of hollow macaroni at the nearly one hundred mice dressed in their blue shorts and blue-rimmed T-shirts who were scurrying into place in front of him.

"Fifth and Sixth Companies! Line up in your squads, and *move it!*"

The plebe mice stretched and leaped in unison. They performed exercises until sweat dripped off their snouts.

All mice could jump, but Ella could really soar. Chester could tell it made some of the fellows mad, but she just smiled and ignored them.

Her nestmate, Shirley—or "Shrill," as she was immediately nicknamed due to her piercing, loud squeak—began to brag about Ella's ability when the detailers were out of earshot.

"Best jumper in your squad. Hoo-yah!" she taunted the male mice.

"She's light. She's got an advantage," Fleet retorted.

Fleet came from a large, prominent mouse family in the big city. He was accustomed to the good life and things coming easily to him. He hated to lose. At anything.

"Yeah, Flip?" Shrill responded gleefully, paws on her hips. "Ella even beat one of the Bobs."

"*Fleet*…my name is Fleet," the white mouse said with irritation.

Brown Bob shrugged. He was the younger brother of Beau Bob and Gray Bob and came from a long line of midshipmice. All the Bobs had gone on to have successful naval careers.

"Good for her," Brown Bob replied with his aura of nonchalant self-assurance.

But he began to leap with greater effort, muscles bunching under his glossy brown fur. It wasn't long before he finally jumped as high and as far as Ella. She shouted and punched him in the foreleg with an easy smile.

"That is one jumper rodent!" Victor pronounced with his thick European accent. Victor had trouble with their language, since he was from another country, but what he couldn't understand, he made up for in effort.

"Victor, come to our nest in your spare time," Dilly joked, making fun of the fact that they had no spare time, "and we will teach you to speak proper American Mouse."

"When I do have the time, Dilly, I will come," Victor politely replied, dark eyes magnified behind this thick, black glasses.

Just then a detailer rushed up, silencing them by his presence and his menacing expression. The plebe mice balanced on their hind legs, staring straight ahead, forepaws at their sides, not making any movement that would draw attention.

"Fall in to your running groups!"

On the first full night of Plebe Summer, the mice had been given the official timed physical readiness test during PEP. Chester had been relieved that he did not experience any twinges of pain in his leg after the squads were sent scurrying around a marked-off course, but he didn't want to push his old injury any more than necessary. He had finished the long run under the required amount of time, though he was bent over, gasping for air, and feeling he might be sick at the end.

Miss Roxie, the tough detailer from INight, stood at the finish point, marking down the times for every plebe mouse. When she recorded Chester's score, she glared into his face.

"How do I know you didn't cheat? I hear you are a rule breaker."

Chester hadn't known if this was a question. He stood rigid at attention, his chest still heaving, stunned that he was being labeled as untrustworthy. His whole life he had been a reliable mouse. He wished he could go back in time and erase the moment he had entered unknowingly into the restricted area. He tried a possible response, speaking with force and volume as they had been taught on INight.

"Ma'am, no, ma'am."

"No? I hear otherwise." She tapped the paper in her paw. "It says here that you reported an injury to the Health Department. Crying already? What are you? A chit surfer? Gonna try to get out of exercise from the start?"

Chester stood in shocked silence. But she continued before he could answer.

"It's mice like you that jeopardize other mice. You're dangerous. You're. Being. Watched." Miss Roxie spit the last three words like bullets, ruffling the fur on his snout.

Chester's stomach had been in an anxious knot as he schooled his globe eyes into a blank stare. Miss Roxie was serious. She really thought he was a conniver and a purposeful rule breaker. That was so far from the truth that it wasn't funny. Who had spread this information among the detailers? Was it the angry mouse from the waterfront patrol? What was his name? Spleen. He had realized then that he was going to have to be very, very careful.

Chester thought about this episode as his running group took off at a scamper, their white T-shirts with the blue trim around the collar already soaked with sweat and blue shorts bunching in damp folds around their tails. He was in a group with the average runners, which was just fine with him. *I'll stand out somewhere else,* he thought. For now he was just trying to stay under the radar of the glaring detailers.

They had been sent on runs frequently since INight. Chester was feeling more and more optimistic about his old leg injury, but he was cautious. *Don't overdo it,* he admonished himself.

They rounded a corner by a marked-off playing field and pounded along a paved road, avoiding bits of gravel. No one wanted to twist an ankle and end up with a chit to get out of physical exercise. Chester knew he couldn't afford to go out with an injury. Those mice had to line up idly by the side of the field, hind legs wrapped in bandages, leaning on sticks and doing nothing but watching the others.

Their detailer shouted out a cadence as he scampered alongside, keeping the group at a swift pace.

"Scurry, scurry, one, two, three. I'm the leader, follow me! One! Two!"

"Follow you!" the plebe mice shouted back.

"Three! Four!"

"Give us more!" the hoarse plebe mice roared.

Dilly inched up alongside Chester, pausing before he passed him by. Dilly had already decided that he was going to enter a long-distance scamper one day, so he was pushing himself.

"How big is this place?" Dilly spoke out of the side of his mouth as they trotted along, chests heaving with effort.

Chester had no idea, but some mice said that the Yard, which was the training compound for the humans and the mice, was acres and acres, maybe even bigger, as in miles and miles. *How far is a mile?* Chester wondered. When he had a free minute, maybe in a couple of months, he thought with decision, he would try to find a map.

One of the plebe mice in his group began to lag behind. Their detailer moved in on the unfortunate mouse.

"Come on, you fur ball, quit your slacking. Mr. Iggy, you are a liability to your shipmates!"

The mouse kept running, grimacing with effort, snout bobbing side to side as he gasped with exhaustion. The detailer kept at him, yelling into his round ear. Chester maintained his pace in the middle of the pack, neither too far forward or too far back. It was a mental game as well as a physical challenge and a matter of survival.

Dilly had moved almost to the front of the group. Another mouse had taken the lead and was running along on all fours with great gallops. Out of the corner of his eye, Chester saw the yellow shirt of the detailer zip by and heard the shouting begin again. Dilly wisely stayed just behind the front mouse.

"What are you, some kind of show-off?"

"Sir, no, sir!" the surprised mouse in front replied.

"Are you trying to bilge your shipmate, Mr. Iggy, back there?"

"Sir, no, sir!"

"Looks like you are!"

The detailer kept the front mouse at a fast pace, without letting him slow down, while leading the rest of the group in a singsong cadence. Their breathing was labored, but they hollered with the required gusto:

*We jogged nine miles, and we ran three,*
*The chief was yelling, "Follow me!"*
*Then we walked two miles and ran eight!*
*Navy PT sure is great!*

The exhausted, overheated mice were led to a puddle, where they quickly washed and rolled up their PT gear into tight bundles as instructed, each exactly the same size. They trotted back to Bancroft Hall behind their detailer, trying not to allow their tails to drag with fatigue.

After first meal, Mr. Bravo hustled the plebe mice to stand at the bulkhead.

"You will be going back outside to begin the process of learning to march in formation. You will be required by the end of the night to stay in step, keep in a tight line, and maintain your bearing. You have five minutes to use the head and clean your teeth and five more to find your gear. Assemble in ten minutes with your parade rifles. Starting now!"

"Sir, yes, sir!" the mice bellowed back.

They dispersed, jostling each other as they trotted in different directions along the passageway to reach their quarters. They didn't know how long ten minutes was because they didn't have time devices, so they flew in a blur of fur.

Chester went to his storage cubby and grabbed his pretzel stick, which had been issued on INight. The midshipmice used the salty sticks in dress parades to represent rifles.

It wasn't long before the story circulated among those mice visiting the head that Bodie had apparently thought his pretzel was a snack and had eaten it on Induction Night.

"How was I to know?" he was reported to have protested, holding his stubby paws up in disbelief.

Chester's heart sunk. *Now we are in for it.*

There were whispers among the group.

Chester heard one mouse muttering, "What if I can't go now? What if I have to go later?"

But he was straining his ears to find out more about the missing pretzel rifle. Bodie's serious mistake was going to impact the entire squad.

Without hesitation, realizing the trouble that would befall all of them when the absent pretzel was discovered, Brown Bob, Bodie's nestmate, took matters into his own paws. The nervous plebe mice peered out of the entrances of their quarters as Brown Bob acted. He slipped behind the nests, skittered down a wire in the wall, entered the human room below in the dark of the night, and managed to secure a few pretzels he found tucked in a closet while the midshipmen slept in their racks. Before the detailers missed him, Brown Bob was back on deck, Bodie had his drill pretzel, plus a spare or two just in case, and the incident was never detected.

Brown Bob's bravery impressed everyone in the squad because no mouse was ever allowed to leave the deck without permission. From the moment they had become plebe mice on INight, it had been drilled into their heads that they could not move an inch without permission. Brown Bob immediately gained the reputation as a brave mouse, and everyone wanted to be his friend.

"I'm surprised Fleet didn't rat on Brown Bob," Dilly muttered out of the corner of his snout as they lined up outside in short rows, ready for instructions.

Fleet was already getting a reputation as a Joe.

"What's a Joe?" Victor whispered from behind.

"A rodent who plays by all the rules without regard for his fellow mouse." Chester spoke so quietly that his deep voice sounded like a rumble. He was picking up the lingo from Ranger. *We have enough challenges without trouble coming from within our ranks*, he thought.

"We call him Joe?" Victor whispered again, trying to figure this out.

"No, we call him Fleet, if we call him at all." Dilly's voice was dry.

Victor looked confused.

"Present *arms!*" the detailer shouted.

The mice quickly snapped their pretzel rifles perpendicular in front of their bodies in a salute as they had been taught. They performed the action over and over until Chester heard a sharp crack nearby. He hoped it wasn't the sound of a pretzel breaking. That could cause trouble. You never knew how the detailers would react. He glanced at his pretzel rifle held rigid in front of his nose. The salt was worn off where his two paws gripped, one above the other.

The instructions continued, the mice marched in step, got out of step, were yelled at, and tried again. The lines were a bit ragged as they tried to look out of the corners of their eyes to stay even with the rodent at the end of their row and not step on the tail of the mouse in front of them. When their drill pretzels slipped off their right shoulders, the detailers barked that they were not holding them correctly. Everyone was struggling, hot and sweaty.

The fatigued mice trotted back to their quarters and were ordered to change out of their white works uniforms and into their camo gear. All were on edge, but Chester felt a shot of excitement when he realized they were being transported to the firing range. He was anxious to see how well he would perform in weaponry.

The first lesson was intense and loud. The detailers hovered over them like angry gnats. The exhausted plebe mice returned from the weapon range limp from effort and instruction. Few felt they had performed well enough. They changed their uniforms once again and lined up in formation on the bulkhead before last meal, their blue books held high in front of their noses.

Chester could not believe that there was room for anything more in the waking hours left before dawn and lights-out, but following last meal, they were sent to a brief to learn more valuable information. Chester thought his head might explode.

After singing "Blue and Gold," as they rushed to prepare for sleep, Ranger reached behind his stack of precisely folded uniforms and pulled out a paper American flag glued to a toothpick. He straightened some creases with his giant paw and then poked the pointy end into a crevice in the floor near his work area.

"Are we allowed to have that?" Chester's voice was calm.

"We're gonna need it," Ranger replied.

"Um…you're not the flag bearer, buddy." Dilly gestured toward the yellow pennant on a stick, which he had just been volunteered to carry for Sixth Company.

"This is for *amnesty*. You'll see."

Chester and Dilly looked at each other. They hoped Ranger knew what he was doing. Any extra items in their quarters that were not allowed would get them in trouble.

"It's us versus the Rodent." Ranger looked with meaning at the other two.

"And who is the Rodent?" Dilly asked.

"Our detailers. Sometimes it's a matter of survival."

"Like what Brown Bob did today." Chester was thinking, staring at the intertwined brush forming the wall of their quarters.

"You got it, brain." Ranger nodded with approval.

"What if he had been caught leaving the deck?"

"He would have been given a conduct offense. That's worth the sacrifice if you're trying to help your buddy."

Chester mulled over this information while he turned to complete a writing assignment that was due at dawn. He paused as he thought about Ranger's words. Covering for each other developed trust and strengthened the bond that was forming between them. *I hope the others know they can trust me*, he thought. He wrote that down, plus a few quick lines regarding his desire to improve at the firing range.

"But never lie. That would be an honor offense," Ranger continued from his corner.

The topic for their first brief had been about the code of honor. The uniformed officer who instructed them had stood on a crate, a slice of light shining down from a crack above, illuminating his glistening globe eyes and row of medals on his white uniform shirt. The plebe mice had perched in tight rows before him, dressed in their white works, their Dixie cup covers held at their sides. Next to him Ella had pitched her firm, clear voice to a yell as they recited together:

> *Midshipmice are rodents of integrity.*
> *They stand for what is right.*
> *They do not lie.*
> *They do not cheat.*
> *They do not steal.*

Chester nodded. He would never commit an honor offense. He wrote that down in his nightly diary that would be collected any minute.

Ranger was still busy rummaging through his belongings.

"Ah, here it is."

In his paw was a strip of white paper with a row of pastel candy dots stuck to the surface.

"Sweet?" he offered.

Dilly's jaw dropped open.

"Sure! Where did you get these? We haven't had a Mouse Mail delivery yet."

"Had them rolled up and stowed in my gear."

Chester shook his head ruefully but quickly took a pale-blue sugar dot. He glanced toward the entrance to their nest and then nibbled the candy with swift, decisive bites. Ranger was the cheese. Dilly chose a green disc, chewed half the candy, placed the other half on his desk while he wrote their required paragraph, and promptly forgot about the remainder of the treat.

"Let's see…what should I say about tonight that won't make them think I've lost my whiskers?"

Ranger took the paper strip of dots, wound it up into a tight roll, and placed it in full view on his desk. He dug again into his cubby, hauled out a large purple gumdrop, and laid it next to the paper strip. He turned to find his nestmates gaping at him and gave them a wink.

"What?" he said with his wide grin, showing two large milky front teeth. "Whose gonna say anything?"

⚜

In the room below the now sleeping mice, Midshipman B. Wise called out the menu, while T. Briggs ran a razor with lightning speed over his face and furiously brushed his teeth.

"Whole-wheat tortillas, crunchy taco shell, shredded lettuce, diced tomatoes...hey, Briggs, not that I mind, but did you open my package of pretzel sticks? Diced onions, sour cream, salsa..."

"Nope, I dropped into my rack last night. You must have done it. Oh man, my shoes are still wet."

B. Wise shrugged. "Must have. Don't remember, but I'm not surprised. Yesterday was a killer...shredded cheese, cookies-and-cream and blondie brownies, sweet tea, milk..."

## CHAPTER 5

# Yellow Alert

⚜

DILLY STRUGGLED TO TIE THE drawstring of his white pants around his slender middle.

"Whose idea was this?" he mumbled as the strings got caught in his claws.

A week had passed since Induction Night, and already the grueling hours and unrelenting regulations had begun to take a toll on the minds and bodies of the plebe mice.

As soon as the detailers awoke the plebe mice, they told them the uniform of the night. The new midshipmice were hopeful that they wouldn't always be required to don the baggy white uniforms because, really, mice didn't wear clothes very well, especially pants. The white works blouse and trousers, which was the uniform of an enlisted sailor, was required to be worn when marching, when reporting for formation, at meals, and when called to briefs, the lectures where important information was shared. Wearing any article of clothing was an added hurdle for the mice. Chester was pretty sure his tail was getting chapped where it poked through the hole in the back of the pants.

"I'm beginning to hate the color yellow," Dilly muttered again under his breath.

Chester didn't take his nestmate's mood too seriously because Dilly wasn't at his finest when he first woke up, but he knew what he meant. He was alert to the flash of the detailers' yellow shirts at every moment. His round eyes constantly scanned his surroundings, and it was making him jumpy. Chester's snout tightened into a grimace as he thought about Dilly's comment. Yellow had always been the color of pleasant things like cheese, butter, crunchy corn snacks, and the occasional dandelion brought in from outside. Chester was particularly fond of dandelions. Bananas too.

But it was best not to think about special food like dandelions, butterscotch cake, round glossy grapes, cocoa powder straight from the bag, and peanuts in the shell.

Chester and his nestmates fell into their usual routine before formation and first meal. They quickly brushed bits of nest material out of each other's fur, straightened their racks into sharp corners, and memorized, memorized, memorized from their little blue books while scurrying around in circles, jumping over each other's tails. The bits of information that had to be remembered from the books were called rates. They would spend the whole summer committing to memory the miles of military information.

Tonight Ranger read the current news aloud, which they were also expected to be able to report during chow call, while Dilly stowed gear, and Chester trimmed his whiskers with quick snips.

"Recent counts show an increase in the mouse population at Bancroft Hall…and that's news?" Ranger interrupted himself with a shrug of his wide shoulders. He then continued. "Vice Admiral Stock intends a visit to the Naval Mouse Academy as part of the distinguished speaker series…no river otters have been seen at the basin." Ranger stopped again. "Good thing about the water rats; now we can have small boat lessons in the sailing basin."

Chester inwardly flinched and glanced at his nestmates. He had not told them about his rescue from the water rat during the winter. He tightened his jaw with resolve, causing his whiskers to poke straight out. He would find a way to prove himself before they knew. He picked up the list of food to be served that night in their dining hall and rapidly called out the menu for the others to memorize.

"Fruit peels, seasoned meat crumbles…"

"Buff chick?" Dilly asked with mock excitement.

"No, not buffalo chicken. Let me finish," Chester said as he continued. "Ketchup soup, trail mix, cheese crackers, cookie chunks."

As he read aloud, Chester straightened the manuals on his desk with one paw. Ranger finished flossing his chunky teeth and refolded his nestmates' clothes the navy way. Dilly swept their floor with the white-bristled blue toothbrush that leaned in a corner of their immaculate nest. They were becoming an efficient team.

On Chester's desk was a letter to his family. Their squad leader, Mr. Bravo, had required them to write a letter home, but they were not actually given the time to do it. Each night, as the sun began to rise outside, he scribbled a few words before lights-out. Chester quickly scanned the square paper, added a last line, and signed his name at the bottom:

Dear Mama and Papa,
So far so good on the leg.
Tell Grandfather that I am in Sixth Company!
My new nestmates are great. Guess what? Dilly is in my nest. The other mouse in our quarters is named Ranger. He is prior enlisted. He has a massive stockpile of candy. Don't know where he gets it. I'll tell you more in another letter.

I'm fine. Please send a cough drop. I'm hoarse because we have to yell so much.

Hello to Grandfather, Allie-Poo, Bean, and the rest.

No time for more.

Love,

Chester

He did not want to worry Mama and Papa, so he skipped telling them that the detailers knew he was the mouse who had been found in the restricted area and that he was now being called unreliable. Best not to alarm them. What they didn't know wouldn't hurt them.

The next night, and the night after that, Chester's squad was led outside with the rest of their company to practice parade drills. Dilly was now the guidon bearer for Sixth Company, so he marched at the front of the lines of plebe mice, carrying the pole with the yellow flag. The plebe mice marched away from Bancroft Hall with their pretzels over their right shoulders, across pavement and grass to the drill field, trying to stay in step. Maintaining a straight line and not locking their rounded furry knees while standing at attention was harder than it seemed, as they were not used to balancing on their hind quarters for great lengths of time. As the weather became sultry, and the moisture from the Severn River made the nights increasingly humid, some of the mice became woozy when marching through the Yard and practicing on the drill field. They took frequent drinks from their acorn canteens or dipped their snouts in puddles when no one was looking.

They were taken to the firing range two more times and to the obstacle course on another night. The pressure was increasing, and the plebe mice knew they still had a long way to go. Chester

found himself living minute by minute instead of hour by hour. He had never been so mentally and physically pushed in his life.

Following their return from a long scamper, Mr. Bravo met Chester's squad and arranged them in a semicircle around him. He was not dressed in his usual yellow T-shirt but wore summer whites, the crisp officer's uniform. Chester noted the gleaming silver Es on the ribbon bar above the left pocket. The little metal *E* indicated Mr. Bravo had earned expert rating in weapons when he was a plebe mouse. *Hope I do too*, Chester thought.

Another detailer, dressed in a yellow T-shirt over his light-brown fur, stopped by to speak with him. "What's the occasion, Bravo?"

"Got a meeting with the dant."

Chester took the opportunity to steal a look at the stars and note the position of the constellations, trying to figure out the time.

"Trouble?" the detailer in the yellow shirt asked.

"Nah, it's all good."

"He's the Cheese."

"Yeah, he's the Rodent."

Mr. Bravo waved the other detailer away and turned his sharp eyes on the group of plebe mice standing rigid before him. Their tails stuck straight out from their gym shorts. They did not twitch a whisker as they kept their eyes in the boat.

"Preacademic testing starts in thirty minutes. This will enable us to group you for classes, which will start at the end of the summer. Some of you may test out of certain classes for the school year if you perform exceptionally well on the written tests."

Several snouts turned ever so slightly to glance at Chester and JP. Round ears often swiveled toward the two plebe mice for suggestions when they were required to think as a group. JP stood motionless, his dove-gray fur just showing under the blue-brimmed cap worn for exercise. Chester kept his bearing, thinking about which subjects he might have the best chance to excel at. He knew what classes were offered from reading through Grandfather's manuals. His nose twitched. He couldn't help but notice that there was a strong smell of sweaty mouse. It did not matter how many showers and baths they took, they were constantly exercising and under stress.

*We all smell like wet rat,* he noted as he thought.

Another detailer trotting by at a good clip stopped when Bravo greeted her with a snout nod. It was Miss Roxie.

"Sheesh, Bravo, your squad stinks," she said with a grimace.

"What's up?" Bravo said, ignoring her comment.

"On my way to the O course. What's the hour, do you know?"

Without skipping a beat, Bravo barked, "Mr. Chester, tell Miss Roxie the time."

Her head swiveled, and she snorted when she saw Chester.

"You!" she spat the word with derision.

Chester guessed Mr. Bravo must have noticed him examining the stars. Their detailer didn't miss much.

"Ma'am, I believe it is zero two thirty, ma'am." Chester's eyes flicked briefly toward Bravo and then to Miss Roxie before he brought his gaze back in the boat. He thought he saw a slight expression of amusement in his squad leader's expression. Miss Roxie looked dumbfounded, and then she laughed.

"You're not supposed to tell them the time, Bravo; that's against the rules."

"I don't break the rules," Mr. Bravo's voice was firm.

She pushed her nose into Chester's snout, "Cheating again, I suppose," she said with a sneer in her voice.

"Back off, Roxie, get your own squad," Mr. Bravo made a joke of the whole thing. "This plebe mouse answered fair and square."

Who was Mr. Bravo defending—himself or Chester? Had their squad leader been told about his rescue from the water rat? Chester drove his long front teeth into his lower lip. Somehow he had to live down that reputation.

The plebe mice were escorted back to Bancroft Hall to change quickly into white works.

Fleet stopped Chester as they all skittered with precision steps down the center of the passageway to their nests. The detailers had stopped by the duty desk and were not paying attention.

"JP and I are planning on testing out of calculations and physical properties and maybe a few other classes. What about you?" Fleet whispered.

"I didn't say that, Fleet," JP commented in a low voice as he slipped past.

Word had gotten around, spread by Fleet, that JP was the great-grandson of a famous rodent naval officer. Fleet liked to be associated with mice in high places and was thrilled that he had been assigned to be JP's nestmate.

"I'm just going to do my best. See what happens." Chester's answer was firm but short. He moved without hesitation through his entrance, relieved to get away from the white mouse.

Ranger, who was right behind him, looked down into Fleet's haughty eyes. "When you need to figure something out, he's the Rodent," he said to Fleet with an innocent expression.

"JP and I..."

They could still hear Fleet speaking.

Dilly began singing, "Anchors aweigh, my mice, anchors aweigh..."

"Stow it!" Ranger chuckled.

"Hey, I was just thinking about JP's very famous great-grandfather!"

Chester gave a slight grin as he slapped a couple pawfuls of cornstarch under his forelegs, jumped into his baggy white pants, and dragged his white blouse over his large ears, yanking the neck opening down when it got stuck. Dilly could be funny, but underneath he was a very motivated, determined mouse.

Right now Chester was determined too—to do his very best on the tests. This would be where he could distinguish himself without being exposed to ridicule in front of the detailers. He was trying so hard to do well without actually being noticed. It was exhausting.

A week later a rumor circulated that they were next to be mobilized to the target field to be tested on weaponry. Third and Fourth Companies had already rotated through, so they were on deck, as Ranger put it. All the mice became tense. This was one of the pinnacle events of Plebe Summer. More than anything, Chester desired to excel at target shooting. If he did well, he would wear two silver pins in the shape of an *E* on the colored ribbon hanging over the pocket of his dress white uniform, which they would all receive at the end of Plebe Summer. The silver *E* for expert, just like Mr. Bravo wore on his uniform, would be a badge of honor, more so than the bronze *S* for sharpshooter. Chester cringed at the thought of no pin in at all. It didn't bear thinking about. Even though the mice were training to work as a team, they were also in constant competition with each other. This would be their first real chance to set themselves apart from their classmates and the first real medal they could earn to wear on their uniform. They would wear these qualification pins for all four seasons as students at the Naval Mouse Academy. And there would be no chance for a do-over.

"Hope I've had enough practice," Ella uttered as she shook out the sore wrist of her right foreleg, her stone-throwing paw.

Chester hoped his target practice at home, especially with catapults, would give him an edge. He and Theo had spent so many nights perfecting their target accuracy, though shooting the large heavy balls that were heaved by the thick rubber-band launchers was another story. At the thought of Theo, Chester was reminded of home. He remembered how Grandfather had shown him paw-throwing techniques using pebbles from his collection and how Papa had created target zones. He tried not to think of home; it made him lose focus. Instead, he turned his mind to strategies for success at the firing range and began to wonder about the abilities of the other mice.

Chester mulled over his fellow squad members. Bodie, coming from a farm, probably had more experience tossing heavy objects like tractor bolts, nuts, and maybe even other mice. He was a brawny rodent but very kind. Probably not the mice. Ranger had traveled all over the world and had had many opportunities to shoot projectiles off the decks of ships. The others he wasn't so sure about. Dilly was a tall, reedy mouse, quick and agile. Victor's background was unknown, as was JP's. Ella might be small, but she was powerful. Brown Bob seemed to be able to do anything. Fleet always talked about winning in contests, but he was also a sore loser, which had become very apparent when their squad lost their first competition against another squad. Afterward Fleet had refused to talk to any of the mice.

"Like it's not partially his fault!" Dilly had said with aggravation.

The night before the testing at the firing range, the mice stood against the bulkhead beside their nests. As the sky outside turned a pearly gray, they remained at attention, ready to retire after another long, hot, and miserable night. Those who had been singled out by their detailers for messing up were especially miserable. A rain shower had moved through the area before dawn, so they had all bathed under a downspout. The smell of damp fur was pungent.

Mr. Bravo, who had become their favorite detailer because he was calm and more often reasonable, shouted at them to count off.

"One!"

"Two!"

"Sixteen!"

The last mouse bellowed, "Forty-five! Forty-five highly moti-vated plebe mice present and accounted for, sir!"

At last Mr. Bravo ordered Dilly to begin the singing of "Blue and Gold" in his fine baritone.

*"Now colleges from sea to sea…"*

Up and down the long line of plebe mice standing moistly at attention, the shipmates sang in unison. Chester's voice was deep in tone, though slightly off-key as usual. No one needed the little blue book anymore; they knew this song by heart:

> *May sing of colors true.*
> *But who has better right than we*
> *To hoist a symbol hue?*
> *For sailors brave in battle fair,*
> *Since fighting days of old…*

***

In the human quarters below, in room 1324, B. Wise and T. Briggs jostled as they dashed through the doorway following PEP. Above their sweat-soaked blue-rimmed T-shirts, their cheeks were ruddy from heat and exertion.

"Wow, it can't be more than seven o'clock, and it's already scorching outside."

"If it gets any hotter, we'll have a black-flag day."

"That won't stop us from exercise; we'll just do it inside one of the gyms."

From the hallway, a detailer bellowed, "Morning quarters formation in five minutes!"

T. Briggs rushed to turn the handles of the shower and stuffed his smelly clothes into a white net bag. Wise could hear his roommate's voice echoing in the shower as he recited:

*The first three General Orders of a Sentry are—first, to take charge of this post and all government property in view; second, to walk my post in a military manner, keeping always on the alert and observing everything that takes place within sight or hearing; and third, to report all violations of orders…*"

"Briggs, I think you have that one down," Wise interrupted with a shout. "We had to arrive on IDay knowing that."

While he waited, B. Wise inspected his white works uniform for dirt smudges and danced from one foot to the other in his shower shoes with nervous energy.

"Oh, Helvetica, I think I've got pen on my blouse!" He grabbed a bleach stick and scrubbed furiously at the spot on his uniform.

His roommate called from the shower, "Wise, how did you do in the AC exams yesterday?"

"Were the academic exams only yesterday? Don't know. Spanish was a breeze; English not so much. Think I did well in Calculus. Briggs! I need the shower!"

"Out. Water's on. Yours!"

B. Wise rushed by with his towel over his shoulder. "Think we'll get more practice at the weapons range?"

"Hope so. I felt pretty good with the pistol, but I need more practice before the rifle quals...that's the one I'm worried about."

"Yeah, me too, the rifle is trickier." B. Wise was out of the shower and toweling off with rapid swipes.

"Hey, I think that was my personal best...a fifteen-second shower."

Through the doorway they heard a detailer holler, "Hit the bulkhead!"

CHAPTER 6

# The Firing Range

❧

CHESTER HAD HIS WHISKERS UNDER tight control. He did not want to betray his tension. "Never let them see your whiskers twitch" was his motto. The mice of Sixth Company were being moved by rolling carts along with the plebe mice of Fifth Company to the shooting range. There were nearly one hundred plebe mice in all. Chester's squad hunkered down on the board in two lines facing each other, tails dangling over the side. They could feel the tightened nerves in the haunches of the mice on either side of them.

The night had begun in the lecture hall with a brief. A senior officer spoke on adapting and improvising, but few of the plebe mice could concentrate. Chester had tried to listen, but he had been too distracted by the upcoming challenge. He flexed his paws as he thought about throwing strategies. He glanced around to see if his shipmates were focused on the speaker. Brown Bob shifted side to side; Dilly curled and uncurled the tip of his tail. He felt the energy mounting in the room. They often attended briefs, squatting in large groups while they were taught important information, but knowing they were soon to be tested for proficiency in shooting and throwing accuracy, a test that they had anticipated ever since Induction Night, brought extra tension, making it hard to listen. There would be no opportunity to change their rating in hurling and discharging missiles once this test was over. Pride, ranking, and two silver pushpin Es for show were at stake.

Chester brought his mind back to the present. Directly across from him on the moving vehicle, Fleet, Victor, and JP stared straight ahead, muttering discreetly behind their whiskers to each other. Victor was telling everyone to relax in his best American Mouse accent.

"Shut up," Fleet snarled.

"We don't need your attitude, Fleet. Everyone wants to do well," JP responded under his breath.

Fleet kept his snout shut, but Chester could see he was angry. His angular jaw was clenched, and his round ears were back and flattened. The night lights glinted off his white fur, which Fleet was quick to tell everyone was silver.

Next to him Dilly whispered, "Good luck!"

Chester nudged Dilly with his elbow, who nudged Ranger, who turned and winked at Ella, who blushed.

"Hey, no fraternization!" a mouse down the line yelled, attempting to make a joke, but a ringing shout from one of the detailers silenced him.

"What is…fraternization?" Victor whispered to JP.

"Romance. Not allowed if you're in the same company," JP replied.

Victor arched a brow. They settled into silence for the rest of the journey to the range.

The mice jumped nimbly down from the rolling carts and were quickly assembled into ranks. Chester's squad was marched at a run toward the testing area. Pyramids of colorful candy sour balls were stacked beside the neat line of rubber-band launchers. Under the bright lights illuminating the field, the mice of Fifth Company were already in short lines behind the launchers, being given last-minute instructions. Leaders from the firing range ran the tests, while the detailers kept the plebes in order and provided extra assistance. Chester's squad was directed to the other side of the Naval Mouse Firing Range, where the paw throw was set up. Little piles of pebbles dotted the strip of earth where the testing would take place. They were each assigned a detailer, who gave reminders about safety, distance, and the proper stance.

To begin the practice session, a striding mouse in uniform shouted, "Clear! Fire!" and a hail of stones sailed across the field to the landing zone.

Chester's practice with Theo and Grandfather had paid off. He was hitting the target nearly every time and beginning to relax somewhat, unlocking his gritted teeth. The small rocks were retrieved, the area swept clean, and then the formal testing began. At the call of "Fire!" the mice began throwing their pebbles, trying to pitch every one into the pit dug at the end of their zone. Chester narrowed his eyes and concentrated with every swing of his shoulder.

"Stop!" the field leader bellowed to the plebe mice.

Silence followed as the detailers walked to the craters dug in the earth and counted the pebbles thrown by their assigned plebe mouse. Chester's instructor, with his distinctive shirt marked *Weapons* glowing in the lamplight, walked slowly to the hole, leaned in, and counted. Stones lay on the ground all over the field. Chester waited.

"Nineteen!" his detailer shouted.

Nineteen out of twenty. Chester had landed enough stones in the target to earn an *E* in the paw throw. He was ecstatic. All around him were mutters of discouragement or restrained paw pumps of elation.

As they were marched across the field to their next test, the rubber-band shoot, Chester overheard two detailers talking.

"Yeah, we were really lucky. A huge shipment of projectiles came in during mail call yesterday. We had a tail sizzle of a time getting them out here," one said, a blade of grass dangling casually from between his two front teeth.

"How'd ya do it?" Both rodents were leaning with confidence on a cement barrier, waiting for the next group of plebe mice to come through.

"Well, we didn't get much sleep. Pushed 'em down the steps."

The two detailers saw Chester's squad approaching in formation, led by their student leader, JP, and pulled themselves up to full height, assuming responsibility. They were very serious about keeping the plebe mice in order and making sure they were properly trained.

Now the shouting of instructions began with greater intensity. Safety was of increased concern due to the power of the launchers and the potential for misfiring. Names were called, and the mice ran at quick time to their assigned places behind a thick rubber band held taut between two spikes in the ground. Every station held a pile of brightly colored sour balls. The situation was so tense, even Bodie did not feel tempted to lick the shiny sugary orbs. The plebe mice were given cotton to stuff into their ears.

The task was explained; they had ten balls to launch with the force of the rubber band. At the other end of the target field was a narrow strip marked off by white lines, the landing zone. All the projectiles had to make initial impact within the white lines in order to count. At least nine out of ten balls had to land in the specified area to obtain an expert rating. Seven out of ten would give them a sharpshooter rating and a bronze *S* pin in the ribbon bar over their pocket. Landing fewer than seven in range meant they would have no letter pin to show off on their uniform.

Chester clenched his teeth and squinted, assessing the distance. At the far end of the field, detailers were stationed wearing protective gear. They would monitor the landing divot of each sour ball. Should it land fairly but roll out of the target zone, it would still count. The detailers donned helmets in case one the projectiles veered straight in a line drive instead of a lob.

The practice began when an upperclassmouse yelled, "Fire!"

Red, white, green, orange, purple, and yellow flashes began arcing in the night sky under the glare of the lights on the huge lampposts. It quickly became clear that strength was not the effective technique here, for the power came from the rubber band. Chester knew he was going to have to think very hard about how far he pulled back on the rubber band and the direction he aimed and then recalculate after every practice shot. This exercise seemed very similar to shooting rocks with his catapults. Methodically Chester adjusted and readjusted as he made attempts with the ten practice balls. At his side his assigned detailer gave encouragement and advice, watching his every move for safety and instructional purposes. When a cease-fire was called, the sour balls were collected with much effort by the detailers, who rolled and kicked them across the field until each plebe mouse had five projectiles at the launching station. Again they were given the opportunity to practice shoot. Around him Chester heard a few cracks as some balls landed upon others already in the field. He readjusted the velocity due to the drag from bits of grass stuck to the candy surface. Every so often the detailers pounded the nails holding the rubber bands more securely into the ground. Even the earth was shaking from the reverberation of the twanging mechanisms. The sound was deafening to their sensitive ears. White-winged moths flew excitedly into the night, a firefly flickered, and even a few crickets hopped out of the restricted area.

With a booming shout, the firing-range instructor called for a cease-fire. He pulled two wads of cotton out of his gray ears and bellowed out more orders. The spent rounds were collected, and now each plebe mouse in Chester's squad stood beside ten sour balls—the final ammunition for their test.

He noticed out of the corner of his eye that Ella was to his left and Fleet on his right. He could not spare the time or effort to locate the others. Chester narrowed his eyes and willed himself to stay focused and calm. *Pack it down*, he thought, determined to keep his nerves in check.

"Fire!" And the test commenced.

Chester chose a green ball and pulled carefully back on the thick band. Slowly, slowly, he backed up, angling the trajectory, and then took a deep breath and let it fly. It soared through the air and landed in a cloud of dust. Chester could not tell if it was just in or just out of the nearest target zone line. He adjusted for his next ball and saw with satisfaction that the red sphere landed squarely in the target area. His yellow projectile was next and then the orange and purple. On and on it went, the thuds pounding all across the field. The missiles were kicking up the dust, so it was becoming hard to tell where all his balls were landing.

He could hear Fleet's voice exclaiming "Yes!" after each of his volleys. He shut out the sound and concentrated. Chester was confident that most of his sour balls were in the target, but he was not so sure about the green one. He held his last shell in his paw, the white sour ball. Chester tossed it to feel its heft, brushed off some dirt and stubble, and then placed it tightly into the rubber band. Pulling back, he squatted carefully, tilted, said a little prayer, and let it go. It sailed high above the field, sparkling in the lights of

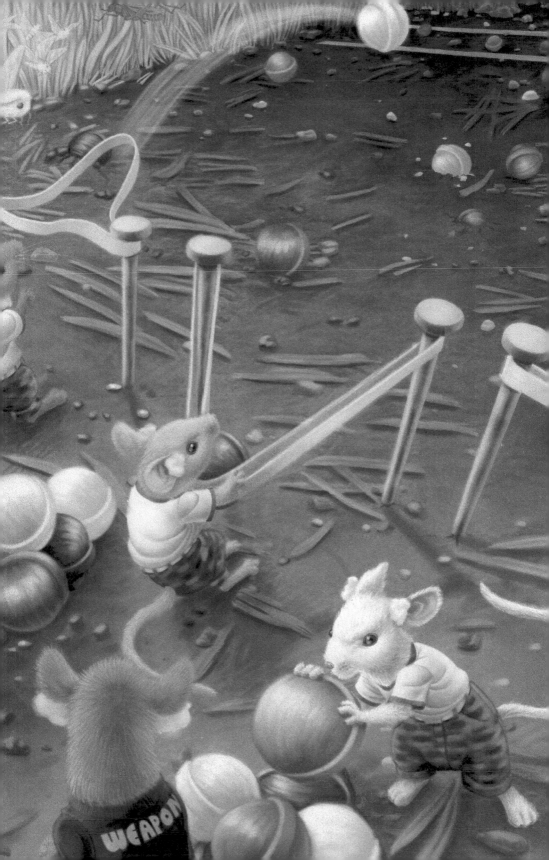

the lamps. Squinting, he could just see it slam into the ground beyond some of his other balls and roll. From where he stood, he could not tell where it had landed. He shielded his eyes with a paw and squinted again. It had definitely rolled to a stop beyond the last line, out of the acceptable range. He would have to wait and see.

Chester fell down onto all fours, let out his breath with a release of his puffed whiskers, and shook his bunched shoulders with a shiver that rattled all the way down to the tip of his tail. He was exhausted, barely registering the continuing load and fire around his station. He breathed deeply again and turned to his right. Several mice down, through the motion of moving bodies, he was just in time to see Ranger pull an orange ball way back, the rubber band stretched to a ridiculous limit, too taut for the distance, and let it fly. It sailed over the field, over the heads of the detailers in protective gear, and disappeared into the night. Chester thought he might have seen it bounce on one of the paved paths. He looked at Ranger, aghast. Had he just thrown in the towel? Given up… bailed out…quit? Ranger turned, caught Chester's bulging black eyes, and gave him a great big toothy grin.

"Cease fire!"

The rattle and reverberations stopped. The mice of Sixth Company stood tensely, pulling the cotton out of their ears and waiting for their scores.

Chester watched his assigned detailer move into the target-zone area, pad and writing tool in his paws, goggles pushed back over his large ears. He was looking about the landed projectiles, counting and recounting with a pointed claw. He made several notations and waited for the others to finish their tallies. Then they walked in a long line spread across the field toward the wait-ing plebe mice.

"Chester."

"Sir, yes, sir!"

"Ten out of ten."

"Sir, thank you, sir." Chester was afraid to show his jubilation, but he was bursting inside with excitement and questions.

The detailer was about to turn and then stopped and leaned in. "That first one was close. The rest were solid and right in the zone. Your last rolled out, but it was a good shot, fair. You earned expert rating." A hint of pleasantness was in his voice.

Chester was overwhelmed with gratitude. "Sir, thank you, sir!"

They were called to line up. Chester moved quickly to get near Ranger in the ranks. As they stood together, Ranger mouthed out of the corner of his mouth, "How'd you do, Ches?"

"Expert." He was trying to sound nonchalant and did not want to brag in front of Ranger, who had certainly not done well.

"Me too," Ranger replied.

"You *did*? How did you…I mean, what about that last shot?"

"Ah, I was pretty sure the others were in. I wanted to see how far that thing could *shoot*."

Chester just stared at him, mouth gaping with front teeth exposed. "Were you *positive* about your other balls?"

"Nope," Ranger replied with another big grin.

Chester shook his snout with admiration at Ranger's bravado.

Just then a tall detailer moved in and shouted at them to be silent. He looked at Chester's name tag. "Mr. Chester, how did you do in the launchers?"

"Sir, expert, sir!"

"Think you're an expert, do you?"

"Sir, no, sir!"

"Maybe you should practice on water rats then."

The detailer moved on. Ranger arched a brow.

Chester shrugged as if to say, "What was that about?" He wasn't going to let a snide joke about his mistake in the restricted area ruin this moment. He was victorious about his scores in weaponry. *I will find more ways to prove myself,* he thought.

The silent plebe mice were marched at a quick trot to the rolling carts.

⚜

Midshipmen B. Wise and T. Briggs had just been led back from breakfast at a smart pace and were now darting about their room, tweaking the sharp corners of their sheets and blue blankets for room inspection. A detailer in the hallway yelled, "Rack races!"

B. Wise groaned inwardly. Rack races was a time filler designed to bridge gaps in between training sessions and also a way to "break" the plebes by testing their patience.

Their inspected beds would be torn apart and tossed on the floor. Then the plebes would have to remake their beds in double quick time and run outside their doors to stand at attention on the bulkhead before the short time allotted by their detailers expired. They would do this over and over, enduring the frustration of watching the detailers rip their beds apart after each round of competition. They rarely won because the detailers usually announced an impossible number of minutes to beat. Still they always hoped they could earn the prize—maybe to be able to sit on the floor, polish their shoes, and converse with each other freely for a few relaxed moments. B. Wise was longing for that little bit of freedom.

As they stood at attention, waiting for the last plebes to dash out of their rooms, T. Briggs whispered to his roommate, "Hey, B, did you hear someone's candy was stolen after mail call last night?"

"Dude, that is not cool. That's an honor offense."

"Yeah, a couple of bags of sour balls. They're making a big deal out of it."

"Who would be so stupid as to do *that*?"

"Beats me."

CHAPTER 7

# Endurance and Friendship

⚜

DILLY DRAGGED HIMSELF OUT OF his rack for room inspection. He was sick as a rat.

It seemed that the minute Fifth and Sixth Companies completed their testing at the firing range seven nights ago, the weather took a turn from hot to hotter and rainy. The mice were dropping like flies in the heat and humidity.

Dilly had barely eaten anything during first meal, drooped back to their nest, and fell into a heap on his rack. He didn't look good: watery eyes, limp whiskers...even his usually shiny short, pale fur was dull. Bodie scampered into their quarters to borrow their brush to sweep his own floor and spied the croaking mouse, now stooping near his mat of fluff.

"What's up with him?" he asked Chester, gesturing with a paw over his shoulder.

"The hack—major sneezes, sloppy snout," Chester answered. "It's been going around. Half the company has it."

Bodie feigned recoil, paw held over his own snout. His voice was muffled through his claws.

"I hear they are quarantining the sick ones in another section of Bancroft Hall. I don't want to go there, though some of the plebe mice are pretending to be ill so they can get out of PEP."

"Chit surfers!" Ranger snorted.

Chester was surprised to hear Ranger rat-talk about any of the other rodents; he rarely did that. He shook his own large ears with derision. Plebe Summer might be exhausting and stressful, but he would *never* want to be known as a slacker. While Bodie talked, they rushed to straighten Dilly's rack, neatly stowing his salty rifle and other gear in his cubby, before attending to their own areas. Dilly slumped in a corner, coughing into his shoulder.

Mr. Bravo pushed briskly into the nest. The four plebe mice leaped to attention. He took a swift look around, twitching his whiskers, noticing their straight racks and shiny floor. The three nestmates held their breath. They needed to pass inspection; if not, there would be very uncomfortable consequences. All four mice were upright on their hind legs, snouts tucked, staring over the yellow shoulder of their detailer, focusing on a speck on the wall.

"What is this, a mutiny? There are too many plebes in this room!" Mr. Bravo said, referring to the fact that Bodie did not live in their quarters.

The four mice did not move. They could be accused of a mutiny because there were more mice than racks in their quarters. If convicted by Mr. Bravo, there would be a harsh penalty. Mr. Bravo's eyes scanned the perimeter and then spied Ranger's red, white, and blue flag poked into the floorboard.

"Ah, I see that you fly the colors of the nation. There is no conspiracy. Get back to your quarters, Mr. Bodie."

The four inwardly sighed with relief. Chester gave himself a little mental reminder to thank Ranger later for his knowledge in bringing the flag.

"Sir, yes, sir!" Bodie scuttled out with the toothbrush.

"You rodents give me hope," Mr. Bravo commented as he continued his tour, looking behind and under objects.

He stopped and backed up until he was positioned in front of Dilly. He looked keenly down his long, pale beige snout for a moment. Chester and Ranger held their breath. They had been trying hard to protect Dilly and keep him out of quarantine. Those unfortunate sick mice were being sent to an unused corner of Bancroft Hall where they were lined up on sparse nests in rows on the floor with the other sick mice. No one wanted to go there.

"The hack?"

Dilly, who had been holding his breath, trying not to cough, exhaled and rasped, "Sir, yes, sir."

Mr. Bravo peered at Dilly's snout and then held out a splayed paw, pushing it close to Dilly's normally moist nose. "Dry nose. A little warm. You want to go down to Health?"

"Sir, no, sir!" Dilly vehemently replied with a strangled cough.

"I should order you to." Mr. Bravo stood, considering. "If you can keep up, you can stay," he finally decided. "But no heroics," he finished and strode out of the nest.

Dilly sagged with relief. Chester and Ranger assured him that they would cover for him as best as they could.

The nights grew harder. Just as Dilly began to feel slightly better and announced that he was going to live, Chester developed a sore throat, itchy ears and could barely manage a squeak. They were all hoarse from the continued hollering and barked replies while running, but this was worse. From the dining hall, Ranger smuggled back bits of dried cereal squares for Chester to keep his strength up and spoons of hot sauce for Dilly to clear his snout. He took his duty to support his shipmates seriously, encouraging them to eat a crumb of food after their rigorous training exercises. At the end of each night as they readied to turn in to their nest, right before mail call and the singing of "Blue and Gold," a detailer examined their paws, fore and aft, for blisters or sores from the demanding exercise. All the plebe mice were pushing the boundaries of their physical limits, but the sick ones were searching the depths of their endurance.

Still they ran, marched, jumped, and stood rigid in formation. It was difficult to memorize the rates and daily chow call with the added fatigue of illness. Dilly and Chester croaked out the Fifth Law of the Navy:

*On the strength of one link in the cable,*
*Dependeth the might of the chain.*
*Who knows when thou mayest be tested,*
*So live that thou bearest the strain.*

"I'm feeling the strain!" Dilly said with a sneeze.

"But we're holding the chain!" Chester joked back with a wheeze. Ranger responded by knocking their furry heads together.

In spite of the extra food Ranger had brought back from the dining hall, both his nestmates were losing weight. This was of special concern for Dilly, who was already a slender mouse.

The mice were weighed every week on a postal scale. Bodie was the only mouse in their squad who had a check mark next to his name due to excessive roundness, but then he was recruited by the Brigade of Midshipmice football team, and they were pleased with his strength and bulk. Now he got to eat extra food at meals.

Dilly was also told to eat extra nutritious foods, but no matter what, he just couldn't gain an ounce.

"I'm trying!" he said after first meal, shaking his snout. "I even ate a second pawful of cold, gloppy oatmeal! Wanted to gag!"

"Hope you didn't," Chester said mildly.

"You were there. Not a sound—wouldn't have dared," his nestmate replied.

The others were slimming down while packing on muscles—all except for Brown Bob, who seemed to stay the same tough, compact size no matter what.

It was a relief when, a time later, the illness passed on through their company, and all were recovering despite lingering coughs.

One evening when the plebe mice were lined up against the bulkhead wearing their stiff white works uniform and holding their Dixie cup covers at their sides, a pacing detailer called out a new set of instructions.

"Listen up, cone heads! Who is already playing a regular sport? Or maybe the question is, who is not?"

None of the plebe mice moved a muscle.

"You rodents are required to be playing a sport. By the end of the week, I want your name on this list." He tapped a paper with his claw. "Varsity or intramurals, I don't give a rat's tail which it is, but you gotta be doing something."

None of the rodents ever felt they were able to keep up with all the requirements, and this just added another activity into their already too full waking hours. Chester thought he heard a few sighs. That was foolish; it was just going to draw attention.

"Choose and attend sign-ups or tryouts by the end of the week," the detailer roared again.

The squads had been given introductions to some of the choices during assigned rotations, sports such as swimming, sailing, and fisticuffs. Chester was excited. He knew exactly what sport he wanted. Grandfather's stories of the first midshipmice floating in the river on boats with billowing sails had sparked his imagination and interest. The sailing team was his goal, and he already had it planned out. Chester also knew that making the team would give him practice time away from regular training with his company. That would be a valuable bonus too.

When the weather was calm, detailers led the plebe mice of Fifth and Sixth Companies down to the river basin to swim laps and learn to sail small boats. Chester kept his eye out for a furry snout with jutting teeth and stubby whiskers. He wasn't going to be fooled by a water rat twice. He remained on alert, eyes skimming the lapping black surface.

*Be cautious, stay vigilant, focus,* he repeated to himself as his limbs pedaled through the water. When the wind blew off the Chesapeake Bay and the rains swept through, they practiced their strokes in the long wave pool inside a distant building on the Yard. The human midshipmen used the indoor wave pool to float small models of ships and learn about their movement in simulated currents. The narrow, rectangular elevated pool was motionless at night, and the mice could easily practice their swimming without the buffeting of whitecaps. When their rolled towels began to smell musty from all the water activity and humid conditions, Ranger showed Dilly and Chester how to drape the cloth strips on the pipes carrying hot water so they would dry more quickly.

Chester's swimming practice in the toilet bowl was coming in handy; it was the silver lining to his frightening leg injury. But the memory of the rescue from the water rat continued to haunt Chester. He was going to have to prove himself worthy in every situation. The expectations were tightening, and it was a tricky game.

In the old arched gym, Chester's company learned the basic intricacies of bare-knuckle boxing or fisticuffs. Brown Bob quickly mastered the skills and became a formidable opponent. Matched against Fleet he efficiently knocked him to the ground. Fleet blamed it on a wet floor, clenching his pink paws and rubbing the white fur on his forelegs as if preparing for another round.

*Sore loser*, thought Chester.

Brown Bob was invited to join the Midshipmouse Fisticuff Team.

JP was adept at anything involving the water and joined the swim team. Victor had always nosed balls around in his home country, so he signed up for intramural soccer. Ella pursued her gift of jumping by going out for hurdles.

Ranger was pretty much good at everything and could not make up his mind, while Dilly, being tall when he stretched upright, decided to play basketball.

Chester and Fleet both tried out for the sailing team. Fleet had earned two silver Es at the firing range, so everyone expected him to join the shooting club. No one knew that Chester, Ranger, and Dilly had also earned the double honor because they hadn't told a soul. None would wear the tiny silver metal letters until the first time they wore their dress white uniforms.

"My rodents have always been yachters. Shouldn't be too difficult," Fleet had announced to Chester before the sailing tryouts.

Chester hoped it *would* prove difficult for Fleet because he just couldn't warm up to that mouse. *He rubs my fur the wrong way*, he thought. But they both passed the written and physical boating tests, which then enabled them to sail small dinghies during Plebe Summer.

The small wooden-hulled boats were simply hewn from wood, having been gnawed into the correct shape by a team of long-toothed mice in the boathouse. Painted blue with a number on the side, the fleet of vessels were all the same. Each had a single cloth sail made from leftover material found in the midshipman tailor shop. The rudder and tiller were fashioned from an earpiece borrowed from a pair of eyeglasses and attached to the stern with an eye screw.

Chester loved to be out on the moonlit water with the breeze blowing the fur on his scruff and billowing his sail. Five nights a week on the water, he enjoyed a brief escape from the stress and tension of the rigid training. He would zip his little boat past the massive human Navy 44s lining the basin and read the names emblazoned on the back of each stern: *Defiance, Swift, Integrity, Gallant, Endeavor, Courageous, Dreadnought.* He soon perceived that sailing was both a mental game as well as a physical challenge and found himself planning how he could excel.

The plebe mice on the team competed in buoy races, cutting each other off in close calls. Chester thrived on the challenge and was even complimented for nicking the hull of another boat as he shot around a turn, narrowly beating the other boat in the race to the finish. *It's like playing a game of strategy,* he thought. Each night as he returned his vessel and tied it up to a weathered beam tucked far underneath the docks of the human sailing vessels, he would deliberately prepare himself to rejoin his squad. There was always the moment when he would need to refocus. Plebe Summer had started out as challenge to be overcome, but now it was a constant endurance test.

One night back in their square, shipshape nest, in the few short minutes they had been given to complete a difficult assignment before lights-out, the three mice swiftly shared sweets that Dilly's mother had sent. Dilly read the note included in the newspaper wrapper while holding a large green candy-coated chocolate in his paw. Chester nibbled methodically on a red candy, while Ranger took great bites out of his shiny blue-covered chocolate, white teeth flashing with enjoyment. They were copying a portion of a famous man's speech that was printed in their little blue books.

They had to write it twenty-five times. This helped them memorize the words.

"I think I knew it after ten. So, Ranger," Chester asked, shaking out his cramped paw, "have you decided what sport you are going to do?"

Chester was still damp around the ears from sailing in the dark, moist coastal Annapolis night. Ranger, who was a very adventurous sort, looked slightly windblown, the growing fur on his forehead pushed straight up.

"Doin' the dive club," Ranger said between bites.

"Scuba?"

"Nah, high dive. I like jumping off high places. Did it from a ship one time. We were at anchor. It was quick going down, but it took a while to climb back up the anchor chain."

He flashed Chester a big toothy grin and popped the rest of the chocolate into his mouth.

⚜

Many hours later, below the nests, in room 1324, T. Briggs and B. Wise were seated at their desks laboriously copying out a paragraph from their blue handbooks. They wrote the same words over and over as a disciplinary measure. Wise had flubbed his rates, as had another plebe, and now their whole squad was suffering. Both were dressed in their blue-rimmed T-shirts and dark gym shorts with the initials *USNA* on one leg. With the small book, *Reef Points*, propped open in front of him, B. Wise printed word for word from a portion of a famous speech titled "The Man in the Arena."

"Sorry, Briggs," Wise muttered for the tenth time, his eyes squinted in fatigue.

"You weren't the only one. How many more do you have to go?" Briggs asked his roommate.

"Too many. I thought I had this memorized, but today I screwed up almost immediately with that yellow-shirted maniac screaming in my face. Let's see. 'It's not the critic who counts, not the man who points out how the strong man stumbled, or where the doer of deeds could have done them better...' Hey, Briggs, this is not just a good quote for military life; Teddy Roosevelt's words are a pretty good description of Plebe Summer."

"Yeah, it seems like he knew our detailers would always find fault. They are always telling us how we could do anything and everything better."

A rustle in the doorway caught their attention. Mr. Bates, one of the Plebe Summer detailers, stepped abruptly into their room, jaw jutting forward, yellow-shirted shoulders pushed back. Both young men leaped to their feet shouting, "Attention on deck!"

"You got a problem with this exercise?"

"Sir, no, sir!" they shouted.

"Let me tell you something. Every minute here is a learning experience. Someday you are going to have to think on your feet in the middle of distraction. You will have to recall information under tremendous pressure. You are not civilians any longer. You are being trained to become warriors and leaders in the military. Got that?"

B. Wise and T. Briggs kept their chins tucked in and postures ramrod straight. "Sir, yes, sir!" they barked back.

"Now, memorize it and write it *twenty* more times each."

Mr. Bates stared with menace before he turned and walked swiftly out of their room. B. Wise waited a few seconds and then let out his breath.

"Sheesh."

They both sat down.

"Wish we had some carbon paper. Let's see, where was I? 'The credit belongs to the man who is actually in the arena, whose face is marred by the dust and sweat and blood; who strives valiantly; who errs, who comes short again and again, because there is no effort without err…'"

On his desk a package from home lay untouched while B. Wise finished writing the president's words until he was required to turn out the lights. The small brown box, stuffed with granola bars, powdered drink mix, cough drops, homemade cookies, and even a few small toys, which had been overlooked by the detailers during mail call, were pushed to the side of his work area. He had looked forward to unpacking the little green plastic army men with cellophane parachutes and giving them a toss from his rack in the dark after lights-out. Instead, he pulled out another lined page and gripped his pen in numb fingers.

"Who spends himself in a worthy cause; who at the best knows in the end the triumph of high achievement, and who at the worst, if he fails, at least fails while daring greatly…"

## CHAPTER 8

# Striving Valiantly

⚜

ALL THE MICE WERE USED to the nightly exercise rotations held outside on the grounds of the Yard, so Fifth and Sixth Companies were surprised when they were kept indoors after being instructed to change into their blue-rimmed T-shirts and blue shorts worn for physical fitness. Quietly, Chester and his squad mates squeezed through an unfamiliar crevice and scurried along for a short distance before they were grouped on a gray floor at the base of a flight of stairs. Their detailer went over the various methods for sprinting and leaping up steps. They all looked around at the gleaming floors and high-turning staircase with interest. Soon they were trotting up and down two flights of stairs inside Bancroft Hall. Ella, who could leap each step without difficulty, turned to grab the paw of any plebe mouse who did not quite make it in one jump and found himself or herself teetering on the edge. Shrill's squad was also assigned to this exercise, and she perched near Ella, grabbing paws and throwing the mice over the lip of the stair with her usual exuberance. Bodie and Ranger were positioned at the top of one metal-trimmed riser, while JP and Chester were at the next, pulling up any mice who were dangling by a nail hold.

Chester grabbed a mouse from Shrill's squad by the foreleg to help him up.

"Give him a yank, Checkers!" Shrill commanded from above.

"Chester," he heard Ella whisper.

When the squads made it to the first landing, they chopped with quick pawsteps and turned sharp corners, reciting, "Go Navy, sir. Beat Army, sir," before approaching the next set of steps. It was the required chant for the human plebes, so it was theirs too. They shouted it as a spirit cheer at every opportunity.

At the top of the stairs, on third deck, they raced down the one-way hallway, hugging the edge of the wall so any midshipmen seeking the head during the night would not see them. All were excited at this glimpse of the interior where their human counterparts lived and trained for this was the first time they had been allowed out from behind the walls of Bancroft Hall into the human passageways. At the next stairwell, the plebe mice hopped down the steps, chopping around the landing with precision turns, chanting, "Go Navy, sir. Beat Army, sir!"

The plebe mice were required to chop around every corner with military movements, while shouting the mandatory phrase. They did the circuit over and over until their hind quarters were numb from the effort. Chester was pleased to discover that he was still pain-free in his left rear haunch. He hoped that injury was history.

Mr. Bravo assembled his squad and continued the training.

"This is not just a physical training exercise but a lesson in the layout of the internal corridors. Pay attention!" he instructed them. "Also, be advised—third deck is a one-way hallway for the time being. We will follow that restriction during this exercise and until further notice."

The humans had been given the restriction as a punishment for an infraction. Mr. Bravo said one of the human plebes had not known his rates, so all were punished. His eyes narrowed into a warning glare underneath his brow whiskers as he shared that information.

"I gleaned this intelligence during a scouting mission last night. We are going to follow the one-way policy as an expression of solidarity with our fellow human officers-in-training."

"That's not fair," Bodie muttered.

As far as Chester was concerned, a lot of Plebe Summer didn't seem fair, but that was how it went. He realized that even if the human plebes wanted to go only two feet to the right outside their door, because of the hallway restriction, they now had to do a complete circuit in the opposite direction, turning left and running down the center of the hallway to the steps, back through the hallway on another deck, to the steps on the opposite end, and chop down the center of their own hallway to their destination.

"Glad we don't have a one-way restriction in our Sixth Company p-way," Dilly whispered to Chester. "I would hate to wake up from sleep and scamper every which way just to get to the head!"

"Roger that," Chester whispered back. It was amazing how much lingo they had picked up in a short time.

As they lined up for formation before midnight dinner, Mr. Bravo informed Chester's squad that after the meal, they would compete in teams in small-craft paddling. They would each be assigned a partner, which would make up a two-mouse team. Each team would be required to fashion a small boat and paddles from whatever material they could find and carry their boats to the Severn River.

"We're going to start by doing some exercises at the water's edge." Mr. Bravo's voice was bland.

"We?" Dilly mouthed the word out of the side of his snout as they stood at attention.

"We will follow the exercise with a run, boats on your backs, to the human swimming and diving center."

Mr. Bravo looked keenly at his squad. Chester realized that he was giving them extra information. He liked Mr. Bravo.

"You will paddle your boats across a pool and carry them back to a finish point to complete the race. Each team will receive points based on when you arrive at the finish line. The lower the points the better. If you come in first, you get one point; if you come in fiftieth, you get fifty points. Got it?"

"Sir, yes, sir!" the plebe mice shouted back.

"When every team is finished, we total the points, and each squad is ranked. I like to win. Do you understand?"

"Sir, yes, sir!"

"The uniform for the exercise is wet and sandy camo gear."

"Sir, yes, sir!"

*Where will we be able to look for boat materials?* Chester wondered. He would soon find out.

During the meal, backs stiff, on the front quarter inch of their seats and looking straight ahead, Chester and his squad mates brought tomato chunks, lettuce leaves, and bacon crumbles with careful precision to their lips. Sharp teeth ground the food with tension. Mr. Bravo asked Victor to tell a joke. They were learning polite conversation at the table and had to be prepared.

"What has twelve legs, six eyes, and three tails and can't see?"

Everyone waited expectantly.

"Three blind mice."

It wasn't very funny, but they all laughed nicely to keep him from having to tell another. Their minds were not on jokes but on the upcoming challenge and selecting an appropriate vessel and objects for their boats and paddles. Chester couldn't help but wonder if Victor knew the whole story of the infamous three blind mice. He had heard about them his whole life. Mama had told it as a cautionary tale while he was still a little pinky in the nest.

"Never stray too far or get into mischief! What were they doing out in the daylight, anyway? Nothing good happens after dawn. Those three blind mice were reckless and up to no good, running this way and that. They ran after a farmer's wife, and she *cut off their tails* with a carving knife!"

Mama's squeak always went up an octave when she got to this part. Chester thought Mama was a bit hysterical regarding the danger. With a little thought and courage, the three blind mice could have handled the situation better. He took a moment to envision how the three blind mice could have gotten out of their predicament. They should have run faster, had a preplanned escape route, and maybe had a weapon or two of their own. He would come up with more scenarios of evasion later. Still he wasn't sure he would ever like to meet a farmer's wife.

He brought his mind firmly back to the present.

They were all thinking furiously, to one degree or another, over the possibilities for the next challenge. Part of the stress of Plebe Summer was never knowing what was going to happen next. Having advance notice was a small nugget of power.

Chester's brain was racing. The key would be to choose a light boat and effective oars. He and his teammate would have to carry the boat a long way. Too heavy, and they would lose valuable time. It had to be buoyant. It had to be able to hold two mice.

*Think, think, think*, he thought.

They were allowed to go back to their nests to change into their camo gear, retrieve their canteens, and use the head for droppings. There was hardly any time before they were scurrying down the pipes and exiting Bancroft Hall by the Dumpsters. Lined up into squads, the plebe mice were silent as the detailers paced in front, announcing the partners for each of the groups. Chester was keeping his bearing, looking straight ahead, trying to blend in and not attract any attention when one of the detailers passed in front of his vision. Above the yellow shirt, the detailer's cone-shaped head swiveled side to side. He had a very long snout with profuse black whiskers. His drab-brown fur, the type found on many field mice, was clipped close to almost nothing on his forehead. He shouted with anger and menace.

"Who taught you to line up? You look like a bunch of hamsters! Who wants to do more push-ups?"

The mouse's veins were bulging inside his bright-red ears. The fur on his neck stuck straight out in sweaty spikes.

*Spleen.* Chester would know that snide voice anywhere. It was the short-tempered midshipmouse who had been a member of the patrol that discovered and rescued him at the waterfront. Chester was a medium mouse, so he was usually toward the back of the ranks. He hoped Spleen would not spot or recognize him. It was hard to shrink down when you were supposed to be standing up straight, but Chester tried.

Mr. Bravo began to call out names. "JP and Bodie, Dilly and Fleet, Brown Bob with Chester, and because there is an uneven number, Victor, Ella, and Ranger will be in this mission together."

They all looked at their partners and nodded. Their first mission. Chester was especially pleased. This was good news. Brown Bob was a tough competitor. His strength and speed would give them a definite advantage. He had not spent much time with Brown Bob. He admired the proficient mouse and hoped the feeling would be mutual.

Just then a small contingent of official mice scurried up. Among them was an artist from the commandant's office who had been sent to make a sketch of each squad for a Naval Mouse Academy publication. Shouts rang out.

"Plebes! In your squads! And look like you like each other."

The mice joined together in genuine camaraderie, though none of the plebe mice were fooled into thinking that they were allowed to lose their bearing. Most were serious, but Victor smiled broadly while the artist drew with quick pencil strokes. Ranger balanced on his hind legs next to Chester and put a paw casually on his back, his other paw draped across Dilly's shoulders. Fleet immediately stretched himself as tall as possible and balanced himself with a white foreleg on Dilly's elbow. Chester noticed Dilly shrug it off as he stepped closer to Ranger. Bodie was told to move to the back, as he was so large. He settled easily next to Fleet, his mottled fur of gray, beige, and brown a stark contrast against Fleets white shiny coat. Ella, JP, Victor, and Brown Bob squatted in front, the latter confidently on all fours, staring without blinking into the eyes of the artist. Chester hoped Mama, Papa, and Grandfather would get to see the picture sometime. Quickly he brought his thoughts back from home—that was dangerous. He could not be distracted—even having this picture done was a distraction. He knew he had to come up with a good plan, and now he also had to stay out of Spleen's way.

The rules were announced. They would have half an hour to scavenge through the plastic bags in the Dumpster to find a suitable craft and paddles. At the end of that time, when they heard the whistle sound, they were to be standing at the curb with the materials for their boats. It was a mental and physical exercise.

A detailer roared, "Begin!"

The plebe mice scampered up over the sides and into the large metal receptacle, tearing into bags with gnashing teeth and ripping claws. There was plenty of room in the huge echoing bin for the mice to rummage and investigate. Almost immediately Chester and Brown Bob came upon two white plastic spoons. They gave each other a snout nod and continued in the hunt. Squeaks and grunts sounded around them, discussions and arguments. Chester spotted a sponge, a green rectangular cleaning sponge. He drew in his breath; this was perfect. A sponge was light, a manageable size, and meant for water; he had seen one next to the sink in the bathroom where he had learned how to swim. He pointed it out to Brown Bob.

"We can both fit on there. It will be a snap to carry. Let's grab it," he whispered.

"Noooo...I'm not sure."

"What? What don't you like about it? We won't have any trouble carrying it. We can both fit on top." Chester realized he wanted desperately to be the one to discover the perfect boat. He wanted to be known as reliable...officer material...admired.

"Look, Chester, I just think we should keep on looking. What about this cup lid?"

"Too small."

"Plastic bottle?"

"Too round. We'll slip off."

"Plastic shoebox top?"

"Way too big."

Brown Bob stared at Chester. "You're not going to agree to anything else, are you? You've got it fixed in your mind that the sponge will be the best. The sponge or nothing." He let out a long whistle through his narrow teeth.

Chester knew his scientific thinking usually came out right. He whispered back, "I feel sure about this. I think we can win. Trust me. If we walk away from this, another mouse will get it."

Brown Bob threw up his paws and shrugged his compact shoulders. "I give up. Let's get this thing done."

They took the green sponge and two spoons out to the curb and waited for the others.

At the sound of the whistle, all the teams were lined up. JP and Bodie had a large circular mayonnaise jar lid propped onto its side and two Popsicle sticks. Next to them, Dilly and Fleet crouched with a blue flip-flop. Two pencils with the ends gnawed into paddle shapes lay across the top. Ranger, Ella, and Victor, with his thick black glasses askew on his nose despite the elastic bands behind his ears, had just hauled up a pink plastic soap container, the kind that held a bath bar and clicked shut. They had it opened and laid out flat, creating two hulls.

"Catamaran." Ranger grinned. The three had two toothbrushes with large bristles and a nail file.

"Rudder," Ella squeaked, pointing to the file.

One of the other yellow-shirted detailers walked up and down in front of them, shouting instructions.

"When I give the go-ahead, you will pick up your vessels and move as quickly as possible to the beach area. You will immediately enter the water and line up in your squads. You will be told what to do from there. Go!"

The plebe mice hoisted their cumbersome boats and carried them in groups as swiftly as they could along the paths to the banks of the river. Chester and Brown Bob found the going relatively easy. The sponge was light, and the spoons stayed on top as long as they kept their steps even. Dilly and Fleet had a little more trouble, since the flip-flop was long and kept tilting, though the rubber surface kept a grip on their paddles.

At the beach they scampered into the water and lined up on their bellies, camo gear soaked and heavy, heads out of the water.

They were told to do push-ups and then hold the push-up position. Mr. Bravo, Spleen, and the other detailers strode up and down the shore, their tails flicking behind them. One after another, the mouse at the end of each line of mice flattened themselves with a dive into the water and wiggled on their bellies under the lifted chests of the mice in their line. Sputtering and grunting, they shimmied in the dark water until they reached the end and formed back up into the push-up position. Then the next plebe mouse would go, until all had crawled, gasping under the soaked cloth and matted fur of their shipmates.

"Suck in your gut!" Chester heard Brown Bob growl at Bodie as he crawled under the mice along the lapping shore, dragging his back legs and tail, pulling himself by his powerful forelegs.

"I am!" Bodie said in an injured voice.

After an agonizing amount of time holding themselves up in the water, they were told to flip onto their backs, which was much harder for a mouse, in order to do sit-ups. The soggy mice shook their heads, flicking the water out of their cup-shaped ears.

Finally they were ordered out and stood aside their boats, toes crusted with sand, gritty bits chafing under their legs and sticking in their fur.

"The race begins now! You will run to Lejeune Hall led by your detailers. You will enter the building and be escorted to the lap pool. From there you will launch your boats, paddle across the water, remove your boats from the pool, and carry the boats outside to the statue of the goat. You will be scored based on your placement. The squad with the lowest total number of points will not have PEP tomorrow night."

They all cheered; missing PEP would be an *unbelievable* relief. No hour and a half of physical exercise. Chester hoped he could help earn that privilege for his squad.

"The squad with the largest total number of points, the one with the slowest times, will do extra evening PEP."

Groans were heard all around.

The shout to start rang out. The teams from Fifth and Sixth Companies lifted their boats and began scampering. Almost immediately JP and Bodie, who were trying to run with the round mayonnaise jar lid on their backs, had to stop to retrieve the lid when it slid off sideways and started to roll. Chester could see others stopping to reposition their boats or change their grips. Some of the vessels were just too heavy. He and Brown Bob soon pulled ahead, the airy, stiff sponge carried easily between them. They kept going, passing group after group. Ranger, Victor, and Ella had to snap shut the lid of their soap dish to reduce the drag as they ran, which made it hard to keep control of their oars. Chester was feeling more and more confident of his choice of boat. They pounded down the paths, sand from the river grating under their legs and shaking off their hindquarters.

Chester and Brown Bob were now at the front of the pack alongside some plebe mice carting a plastic sandwich container and another group of three in single file with a foot-long ruler balanced across their backs. These rodents were on the track team and fast. Chester was an average runner, but the sponge was weightless, so he and Brown Bob were making excellent time.

The leaders arrived at the building and entered through the designated hole. They were pointed to the pool area with shouted directions, their claws clattering and skittering on the cement floor. The smell of chlorine was powerful as they rounded a corner and found themselves approaching the pool at a dead run. The detailers were standing opposite each other, swinging their paws toward the deep water and barking, "Run, run!"

Chester and Brown Bob reached the edge at the same time as the two other teams from Fifth Company. They tossed the sponge to the ground, grabbed the spoons, and shoved their boat into the water, jumping on simultaneously. They stood on either side for balance and began paddling furiously.

They had moved only a short distance when Chester began to feel water beneath his toes. The hard surface was becoming soft, terribly soggy, and difficult to stand on. He was stunned. The sponge had completely soaked up water.

Behind them they heard splashes as other boats were tossed into the water. The team on the sandwich container rowed by maneuvering their boat with two stiff orange peels. Brown Bob and Chester rowed harder, but they were not moving very fast. It was getting increasingly difficult to paddle, and the water lapped occasionally around their ankles.

Brown Bob growled, "Chesterrrrrrr."

Chester tried to push his spoon even harder through the cool water. He *had* to make this work. Boat after boat began to pass them, though he could still see the ruler team having some problems of their own. They were trying to row the ruler like a crew boat, but it wasn't working. The trio had to jump in and tilt the water off the surface of the stick every so often to keep the ruler afloat.

Across the pool to his right, Chester saw Bodie and JP wielding their red-stained Popsicle sticks, as the mayonnaise lid twirled round and round in the stirred-up water. JP was yelling something to Bodie, which must have helped because they stopped spinning and started to move forward.

Chester and Brown Bob were not even halfway across the pool and had slowed to a horrible, creeping pace. Brown Bob threw his spoon on the sponge, where it landed with a slight splash.

"Brilliant," he uttered.

If ever he needed to think, it was now. Chester felt panic rising and struggled to pack it back down.

"In the water!" he shouted and jumped off the back, leaving his spoon lying across the top.

He began swimming from behind with all fours, nudging the boat with his snout. Brown Bob looked around at the swarms of boats passing by and jumped in after Chester. Taking their weight off the sponge kept it from dipping below the surface. They pushed and swam all the way to the other end, gasping, and snorting the water from their nostrils, snouts up, whiskers plastered to their necks.

The worst was still to come. They had to drag the sodden sponge from the pool, heave it to their backs, and begin the return run. The soaked sponge was much too heavy to be carried. Brown Bob was so disgusted that he squeezed out from underneath and stalked off into the dark. Chester tried to carry the vessel on his own. He was determined not to fail. For a few agonizing paces, he dragged the green soggy rectangle, his belly scraping on the ground. It was impossible. He slid out from underneath and looked at the wreck of his hopes. It was a sodden mess. To either side, he was aware that teams were still running by with their boats held between them or balanced on their furry backs.

A detailer passed by with a clipboard, his thick tail hissing on the wet cement floor. Chester shot a look and then quickly turned his snout so that only the back of his ears could be seen. It was Spleen.

"Pathetic," the drab mouse uttered as he continued by without stopping.

Had he recognized him? Chester could just picture his coarse snout, nostrils flared with loathing.

Chester's mind raced. Suddenly he leaped on top of the sponge and started jumping. He jumped and pounded with his heavy hind paws until the moisture began to ooze in gushes onto the floor. He felt a jolt next to him, and the sponge heaved. Brown Bob was *back*. They both jumped and leaped until enough water was out that they could drag the sponge inch by inch out of the building and across the grass to the statue of the goat.

Most of the teams had already arrived at the finish point. Gratefully Chester realized that they were not the last. The three mice from Fifth Company with the ruler vessel had to stop too many times to keep it from sinking. They were not last either, but they were close. Two mice had lost their boat to the bottom of the pool. Several boats had sprung leaks. Still Chester and Brown Bob had finished toward the back of the pack. Chester moved forward in the throng of mice finding a place to sit, wondering what he should say.

Without a word Brown Bob turned and stomped away.

Chester hunched down amid the swirling horde of mice, feeling exhausted and alone. In the distance the bells from the tower tolled. No one was calling them to attention. The detailers were still calculating the places of each team on a master list. Many of the mice dropped to the ground to rest. Across the grass Chester could see Dilly at the center of a group of laughing mice. He could just hear bits of his story.

"So we switched places, and I sat on the front, paddling side to side. Fleet moved to the back…his weight kept the flip-flop toe from going under. It never took on water after that…yeah, great naval architecture…the *best* shape."

Dilly was gesticulating, and Fleet was actually smiling at him. Fleet was *grinning*? But then he liked to win. They must have done well. Chester could not believe how wrong it had all gone. Visions of being recognized as a leader, becoming friends with Brown Bob, and making up for his mistake in the restricted area of the waterfront while a civilian mouse went *pop, pop, pop* in his head. His first mission was a failure. He had been so sure the sponge would work.

Under a streetlamp he saw Victor, Ranger, and Ella sitting in their two-sided pink soapbox as if it was a boat on an evening cruise. They were leaning backward against the sides, content, slapping each other's paws.

Chester felt like eating dirt.

⚜

Midshipman B. Wise hustled into his room, shedding heaps of wet and sandy clothes onto the bathroom floor. Tilting his head side to side, he rubbed his neck, turned on the water, and raced into the shower to clean the river debris from his body and simultaneously rinse his camouflage pants. He tipped the damp, gritty sand out of his athletic shoes and left them to dry.

"Phew, these stink! How did you do in combat competition this morning, Briggs?" he called out from the shower to his roommate.

"My squad did pretty well in the log carry. I could not believe how heavy that thing is! My arms are still aching. It's like a telephone pole! It took nine of us to lift, carry it, and try to beat the time of the fastest squad. We did okay. We worked as a team, that's for sure. Did better in the Zodiac course. You?"

"Some people don't know how to carry a boat," B. Wise called out. "I'm not so sure about teamwork in the Zodiac races. Those inflatables are cumbersome. Once we heaved the boat onto our shoulders and ran, it was tipping all over the place. When you have plebes of differing heights, *some* people are carrying *all* the load. Then another squad pushed too close and kept squashing my head

116

between our boat and theirs. *Boing, boing.*" He imitated the movement by slapping his hands on both sides of his head.

"Maybe it will bring you to your senses," Briggs joked. "Hurry, Wise, we have formation in a few minutes. Then what?"

"Well, like you, we put the Zodiacs down at the edge of the river, laid down in the water, did exercises forever, and then pushed the boats in and paddled around a course. I tell you, it was obvious who has never rowed a boat but *insisted* they had. It was frustrating."

"Did you tell them what to do?"

"I tried, but it's hard when you're in the middle of a race. We were all yelling and needed to win."

## CHAPTER 9

# In The Arena

❧

THE SOUND OF CHESTER GRINDING his teeth was beginning to become irksome to his nestmates. Mice tended to grind their teeth when they were delighted or stressed. Dilly and Ranger knew it wasn't because he was happy. When Chester turned his back to stow his gear, Dilly caught Ranger's bulging eyes, shrugged, and stuck his claws in his pale ears.

Since the vessel challenge, Chester had been going through the motions, but he was mostly preoccupied and withdrawn. He did everything correctly: learned the required professional knowledge by heart, carried his pretzel rifle with precision, marched in formation, and ate and spoke properly at meals. He did what he was supposed to do, went where he was supposed to go, and followed directions. But he was miserable.

Chester could not admit how shocked he was that he and Brown Bob had done so poorly in the vessel challenge.

The day after the boat race, the winning squad had been excused from evening PEP, while the losing squad endured an extra hour of exercise. Chester's squad was safe, but he felt responsible for not pulling his own weight. He especially felt as though he had let Brown Bob down. He had wanted to excel, show the other rodents he was worthy. He had been so sure their boat would work. Now he felt like...

"Vermin," Chester muttered, not realizing he had spoken out loud.

"What?" Dilly asked.

"Nothing," Chester replied.

Chester was discouraged. How hard it was to stand out among a sea of mice who were all gifted and proficient! He had let his squad down. He had let himself down. In the pit of his stomach, a worry gnawed and grew—was he the weakest link? He had never felt like such a failure in his whole life.

With a sigh he polished his silver belt buckle and gave a little preoccupied smile when Dilly made a joke. Ranger grabbed him by the head and rubbed the knuckles of his paw across the growing stubble between Chester's ears.

"What's up, rodent?" His tone was bracing.

Dilly and Ranger did not realize how much Chester's poor performance in the boat challenge was eating at him, but they knew that something was wrong with the normally even-tempered mouse.

"Fidelity is up, and obedience is down..." Chester began.

"That's not what I meant."

Chester ducked out of Ranger's grip and went back to swirling the cloth over the metal. Dilly and Ranger gave each other a look and returned to their duties.

*Squeak, screech,* continued the sound of Chester's teeth.

It was a Sunday, and the plebe mice were given an opportunity for quiet meditation in various locations throughout the Yard. Many took advantage of this time for reflection, though it was not required. Chester decided to join the mice going to the chapel. He added the required black kerchief and special cover to his white works uniform.

Their detailer escorted them on a silent march down the main straight path through the trees on the Yard. Plebe mice were not allowed on any curved walkways. They would earn that privilege in their second season. It was just one of the many rules that created difficulty and separated the plebes from the upperclassmice.

They passed the chapel, its high, rounded green dome with cupola gleaming in the moonlight. From the path Chester could see the entrance, the massive front door flanked by two inset stone pillars, which were topped with an inset cross and crowned by an ornamental half-circle roof. As the plebe mice were being led around the side of the chapel to a small space in the wall, the white steps and front door seemed to beckon to him. Before he could reconsider, Chester slipped away from the group and scampered up the wide stairs that narrowed toward the top without the detailer noticing. He squeezed through a small crevice in the stone and soon found himself in a vast room with a high ceiling. Staying close to the walls, he skirted past benches and alcoves, scurrying along on a soft blue carpet, until he stood before a massive carved wooden wall topped with colorful glass. He sat, twitching his tail, thinking and making occasional ear-piercing, grating sounds with his teeth. The cavernous space was quiet and dark.

He had always *known* Plebe Summer was going to be difficult. They had been *told* they would fail. But he had not expected it would be as painful as this. He smarted with failure. Nothing in his young life had prepared him for what he was feeling. Was he even cut out for a naval military career? Did he have the makings of an officer? For an instant he wondered if he should go home.

Behind him he heard a cough and a low voice clearing its throat. "Ahem, excuse me?"

Chester whirled around in a panic. He was not supposed to be here. If he was discovered, he would be in such big trouble that the incident in the restricted zone would seem like nothing by comparison.

Sitting serenely on a wooden bench was an elderly mouse with small wire-rimmed glasses. He had a leg crossed and observed Chester placidly.

"I couldn't help but notice you there…plus, your teeth were making quite a racket. Can I help you with something?"

Chester didn't know what to do. He should leave, but he wasn't quite sure who this well-spoken mouse was. He did not have a uniform or any identifying mark. He was in civilian fur. Maybe he was a custodian.

"No, sir," he replied. "I was just sitting here thinking." It was all he could come up with to say.

"Ah! I have often sat here to think. What are you thinking about?"

Chester sighed, and his shoulders slumped.

"If you are worrying, this is the place," the mouse offered kindly.

What did it matter if he told this stranger? He looked around and lowered his voice. His front teeth sagged down over his lower lip.

"I'm a plebe mouse, and I'm wondering if I belong here." His breath came out with a whoosh. "I made a big mistake, and I feel like I don't measure up. I let myself down."

"This sounds serious." The old rodent paused and rubbed his whiskers. "Did you lie?"

"No!" exclaimed Chester.

"Rat somebody out?" The elderly one laughed a little at his own joke.

"No!"

"Bilge one of your classmates by trying to make them look bad? Steal? Cheat on a test?"

"No, no, *no!*" Chester was horrified at the possibilities.

"Well, then what did you do?" he asked, rubbing some dust off his glasses.

Chester took a deep breath and unburdened his worries as he hadn't yet been able to do with his nestmates. Somehow it seemed easier to tell a stranger he would never see again. He told the kind mouse about the way he had been heavy pawed in choosing the race vessel, how he had overridden Brown Bob's concerns, and how it had all gone so terribly wrong. Brown Bob had walked away from him, and he had almost been the cause of his squad having to do extra running, marching, and calisthenics.

"But they didn't?" the mouse asked.

"No," Chester replied.

"Just checking. So you know a lot about sponges, do you?"

"No, not really. Not at all. I mean, I didn't know a sponge would sink like that."

"Absorbency," the mouse muttered cryptically.

Chester looked at him quizzically.

"You will learn about absorbency in your physical properties class once the academic year starts."

Now Chester's guard was up. How did this old gentlemouse know what classes he would take? In spite of his fear, he was comforted by the old mouse's tone and wanted to hear more of what he was saying. Warily he continued to listen.

"So you didn't know the sponge would fill with water. Whose fault does that make it?"

"Mine, sir," Chester said simply. "I know that."

"Did your friend, Brown Bob, tell you it would soak up the water?"

"No," Chester said. "And believe me, I don't think he considers me a friend."

"Did he tell you so?"

No, but he hasn't spoken a word to me since. What if I were to make a mistake like this again when leading other mice?"

"I suspect you will never choose a sponge for a boat again." The mouse chuckled. "Are you going to be leading mice next week?"

"No. Anyway, I doubt it," Chester replied sincerely. "What a mess I have made of everything," he finished under his breath.

"*Everything?*" The old mouse let the word settle before he spoke again. "So maybe you'll be taught what you need to know during that time to be an effective military leader."

Chester squatted and thought about the conversation. He was staring up at the colorful prisms of glass.

"Still thinking about going home?" the old gentlemouse finally asked.

"No. How did you know?"

"Everyone thinks about leaving at one time or another. Just so you're not considering Tango Company."

Chester shook his head. He knew that any mouse who expressed the desire to leave the Naval Mouse Academy during Plebe Summer was placed in Tango Company so that their negative attitude wouldn't affect the others. They were given time and counseling to rethink their decision while being kept separate.

"Just checking. Come on, I'll walk back with you so you don't get into trouble."

Chester glanced at the old gentlemouse. Who was he? He reminded him a bit of Grandfather. The bells in the tower were chiming, and he knew he had to return.

They were strolling slowly back to Bancroft Hall, the older mouse looking up at the stars, sniffing the air every so often.

"'On the strength of one link in the cable…' What's the next part?"

"Dependeth the might of the chain," Chester replied without thinking.

"You were a strong link, wouldn't you say? What was your name again?"

"Chester, sir."

"Excellent name! Full of history! A human admiral was called Chester…last name of Nimitz. Tell me again about what happened when the sponge took on the load of water."

Chester didn't mention that his grandfather's name was Nimitz. He retold the story of pushing their boat across the pool and jumping on the sponge to splash out the water.

"Sounds like you worked very hard!" the old mouse said admiringly.

"I worked my tail off!" Chester gave his tail a little swish.

"Whose ideas were those to salvage what you could of the race?"

Chester thought for a moment. "Well, they were mine."

"Good problem solving. So tell me, Chester, what would have made you a stronger link?"

"Maybe if I had worked together with Brown Bob instead of insisting on my own way?"

"I'm sure you will in the future."

Chester remembered his interview with Admiral Bilge. He could hear his own voice answering with confidence, "I work hard and don't give up."

A fresh breath of resolve caused Chester to pull his shoulders back and extend his tail straight out behind.

The old mouse spoke next to him, "Now tell me about those spoons. They sound like a splendid stand-in for oars. How did they work in the water?"

The two walked on until they came to the massive gray stone building. The older mouse looked keenly into Chester's large black eyes.

"The choice is yours. It may seem that you go from failure to failure, but the chain will only grow stronger. Bear the strain... trust me."

With a little wave, he ambled off into the night toward the wing that held King Hall. Chester realized he had never asked his name.

He returned to find Dilly shoving laundry into a net bag, which he closed with a large silver safety pin. Ranger was stooping to peer underneath his desk, reaching to retrieve an extra stash of sweets.

Dilly glanced up from his rapid movements. "Hallooo." His welcome was brief.

Chester realized that his absorption in his problems had affected his nestmates. He thought about the old mouse's recommendation to be a strong link in the chain and knew it mattered here too.

"Sorry I've been such a rat," he offered.

Ranger straightened up to his full height and pushed back the wave of fur growing between his ears. Snatching his Dixie cup cover from his desktop, he asked, "What's going on, Ches?"

It was hard for Chester to admit his worries and shortcomings. He wanted to be admired, not pitied. His glossy eyes shifted around the nest.

"Uh...I'm making more mistakes than I thought I would. I started to feel like I wasn't measuring up." His deep voice was grave. He took a breath—it was time to share the big black mark hanging over his head regarding the water rat. They were bound to find out anyway.

"I didn't tell you rodents, but I got into trouble before I came here. I was warned I would need to watch my step. I accidently took my training into the restricted area and had to be rescued from a water rat."

There was silence in the nest, and then Dilly and Ranger burst out laughing, clutching their furry bellies, their long front teeth chomping with each guffaw.

Chester didn't know whether to laugh or be offended. "I almost didn't get in!" he yelled over their laughter, trying to explain himself.

Once they had pulled themselves together, Dilly rested his short foreleg on a support beam and replied, "You think you are the only one with a story? I applied to the Naval Mouse Academy when my horde was living on the West Coast. I got wait-listed. Didn't make the first cut."

"What did you do?" Chester was imagining what that would have felt like. He would have been devastated.

"I went to a small civilian mouse school near my home named Gorgonzola. I knew I needed to remain competitive."

"Gorgonzola?"

"Yeah, it's a cheese school. I took some classes, reapplied, and hoped. I was determined to be accepted here."

Ranger and Chester waited silently until Dilly finished his story.

"I really liked it there. Good school, learned a lot about cheese, but my heart was here. My family understood what this appointment meant and helped me increase my chances at being selected. We moved here in a packing crate so I could meet the admission committee. Mama and Pop really put themselves out for me."

Chester thought about his own family. He realized how much everyone had supported him and helped him after his leg injury—he didn't want to let them down.

Ranger spoke up for the first time. "I was on a dairy farm on a great spread of land when I got my letter that I was accepted. But things didn't go as planned. I ended up going in a different direction for a while...enlisted and served on a ship."

Chester knew there was more, but Ranger was choosing not to share for now. He was an enigmatic mouse.

"Did you stay clear of the farmer's wife?" Chester couldn't help asking.

Ranger knew what he was talking about; he too had heard of the three blind mice.

"Nah, that's an old mouse tale, a field legend. Saw the farmer's wife, didn't chase her, no carving knives. See? Still got it." He swished his muscular tail.

Chester smiled at Ranger's bravery and got back to his story. "Sorry I've been such a rat," he apologized again.

"More like a gerbil," Dilly broke in.

"I know it's easier when we pull together," Chester said, ignoring him.

"Yeah," Dilly joined in. "Who's going to help that big rodent there with physical properties if you check out on us?"

Chester laughed gratefully.

"But I have to tell you one more thing. One of the midshipmice in the patrol who found me in the restricted area was Spleen. He wasn't very nice. I'm trying to stay out of his way."

Dilly and Ranger both grimaced at the mention of the unpopular detailer. Spleen had developed quite a reputation for being harsh and quick tempered.

Shouts rang out in the passageway. The free time had been but a short respite, for they were immediately mustered to a lecture hall to hear a brief on service and duty, which was to be delivered by a high-ranking mouse official from the navy. They were dressed in their white sailor blouses and Dixie cup covers for this special occasion. The plebe mice were led into the large open area underneath Alumni Hall and grouped in their companies, with yellow flags flying at the lead of each marching unit. They hunkered down in front of the raised platform. A light shone through the ceiling of the space, casting a beam upon the empty stage. Four mice in dress uniforms stepped smartly up and strode across the wood. An officer shouted for attention, and the plebes rose to their feet.

The superintendent of midshipmice stepped forward and spoke briefly about naval history, using his sword as a prop. This particular sword from his collection was orange and had originally been a snack pick scavenged after a reception held at the human superintendent of midshipmen's residence. Most likely it had once skewered an olive or chunks of cheese on a hors d'oeuvres tray. He held it high, letting the light glint off its shiny surface. Then he introduced the special speaker.

"And now, midshipmice, give your attention to our guest, Vice Admiral Stock."

A slim mouse rose and stepped confidently to the front edge of the platform. With a paw he quieted their applause and motioned for them to sit down. A bright reflection shone off his small glasses. He stood in his dress whites, paws clasped behind his back, chest full of ribbons and bars. He gazed around at the sea of small furry mice in their white blouses, caps held in their laps.

A sick feeling of recognition rose in the pit of Chester's stomach. The vice admiral was the gentlemouse from the chapel.

"It is a pleasure to be here. I remember when I was a plebe mouse at the United States Naval Mouse Academy. It does not seem that long ago."

Chester's stomach was now in his throat, and his head was spinning. He would know that voice anywhere. He had been spilling his guts to Vice Admiral Stock.

"I spent some time walking about the Yard tonight, visiting some of my favorite places."

Chester was rapidly thinking. The elderly mouse had walked off toward King Hall. He probably had had a meal with the commandant and superintendent of midshipmice. If he had shared the story of their meeting in the chapel, Chester was toast.

"I was going to speak to you tonight on the subject of duty. But I have changed my mind. If you will bear with me, I am going to talk to you about failure. Failure and character."

Chester shrunk down to the floor. Victor glanced over at him, black glasses peering in the dark. Chester's teeth began to squeak.

"What does it say in your blue handbook? Follow along with me. 'Diligence in doing your job, honesty, loyalty, and hard work are what mold a mouse into a rodent of character.' What happens when you have been performing your duty and it leads to failure?"

He had the attention of all the mice in the room. Every ear was rounded and turned toward his voice like little radar bowls.

"Character is taking full responsibility for your actions! Character does not point a claw at others and say, 'It was his fault.' You make an error, you own it." Vice Admiral Stock paused to let his words sink in.

"I met a plebe mouse today."

*Oh no, here it comes*, Chester thought. His tongue was dry and stuck to the roof of his mouth behind his large front teeth.

"His name was…let's see, it was, it was…his name was Brave, I believe. I am going to call him Brave because he told the truth without excuses."

Chester exhaled.

"He was brave in defeat. He had made a mistake, and he owned up to it. Now he has the opportunity to learn. If you don't know about something, learn it. Your personal success here is often going to be learned through failure. How do I know that? Because I failed, and I saw other strong mice fail around me. You know who continued on? Who succeeded? The ones who failed with integrity."

The mice were quiet, quiet as a...well, you could hear a pin drop. Vice Admiral Stock began to pace back and forth across the platform.

"Often, you are going to come up against two choices: the easy path and the difficult path. Which will you take? The easy path is ducking into the nearest burrow hole. The difficult path is chewing a new hole with tooth-numbing, tail-breaking effort. The easy path is not trying or putting the blame on your shipmates. The difficult but rewarding path is being selfless and being morally, mentally, and physically fit. When you fail, you get back up and keep gnawing at that hole. Gnaw, gnaw, *gnaw*. Which will you choose?" The vice admiral tapped the seam of his pressed white pant leg with a thin claw. In front of Chester, Bodie's big incisors were chomping up and down.

In his heart Chester knew, *I don't want to give up. I'm meant to serve and protect the horde...and I want to make Grandfather proud. I choose the difficult path...I choose the difficult path.*

Vice Admiral Stock raised his gentle voice to a commanding boom. "What is the Fifth Law of the Navy—repeat it with me!"

The sea of mice began to shout together:

*On the strength of one link in the cable,*
*Dependeth the might of the chain.*
*Who knows when thou mayest be tested?*
*So live that thou bearest the strain!*

He surveyed the crowd of plebe mice, his small glasses glinting in the scattered light filtering down from the cracks in the ceiling above.

"Bear the strain, shipmates! Accept the hard work! Your future leadership must reflect the highest standards. You are just as accountable for your successes as you are for your failures, and believe me, you will have both."

Every mouse was leaning forward. The vice admiral lowered his voice again, gesturing with his paw.

"When you achieve a goal, the bar is going to be raised higher. When your efforts come to naught, you will learn from that disappointment and keep pushing forward. This will mold you into the type of leader who will motivate others to follow… not only your command but also the same path—the difficult but honorable and rewarding path."

The old vice admiral stood gazing at the sea of whiskered faces hanging on his every word.

"And I have one last thing to say…Go Navy!"

The young mice leaned forward and screamed, noses pointing forward, whiskers angled back, "Beat Army, sir!"

The rafters rang with their voices. The entire brigade was energized by the stirring words of the vice admiral. They scurried back to Bancroft Hall with renewed vigor. Every single mouse was tired, hoarse, and sweating in the summer heat. They had been pushed hard, tasted failure, and often felt its sting. Most were lifted up by the encouraging call to bear the strain with courage, but some mice privately remained unsure of their place at the Naval Mouse Academy. And among their ranks, a few requested to go Tango.

"Heard J. Tidwell's going Tango. He was moved out of Third Company today. He wants to leave," T. Briggs told B. Wise quietly as they rapidly prepared for bed after a long day of being pushed and pulled in more directions than they could count.

B. Wise was scrambling through his closet looking for something.

"It's got to be here…where is it? *Where is it?* Why is Tidwell checking out?"

Briggs pulled out exercise shorts and T-shirts, sniffing them to see if they were too smelly to be worn again. He shrugged and set them aside.

"Don't know. No one has spoken to him. But I heard he decided he was not cut out for the military. Doesn't like the life."

"Well, right now who does?" Wise retorted. "He's a fool to leave. Briggs, come on, man, have you seen my drill rifle lock? I know I had it secured to my gun locker!"

Just then a detailer walked into the room. Dangling from his finger by the *U*-shaped end was a round silver metal lock with a black dial.

"If I can unlock it, you lose it, Mr. Wise."

B. Wise stood stiffly, his jaw set. "Yes, sir."

"Found the combination to your lock too easily. It was right where anyone would look for it. Why did you leave it in the drawer of your desk so close to your gun locker?"

"Sir, no excuse, sir!"

"It's a very dangerous thing to leave your gun accessible like you did. The lock is mine now. You have a day to find another."

The detailer turned and walked out of the room.

B. Wise looked at T. Briggs and muttered, "I'm sunk."

He had tucked the paper with the combination written on it in the back of his drawer. With all the other memorization they were doing, he was afraid he would forget the numbers. It seemed he was always behind, always racing to catch up.

"Do you have an extra lock, T?"

"Nope, I'm down to my last one too. The Lock Monster has the other one."

The Lock Monster was a monstrous mass of all the connected metal combination locks that had been collected by the detailers and fastened together.

"I'm going to try getting away with a bike lock," B. Wise decided.

They both pulled on their gym shorts and blue-rimmed T-shirts and then dashed into the hallway to stand at the bulkhead.

"Man in the arena!" shouted one of the detailers who was busy walking up and down before the young men and women who stood at attention, chins tucked, eyes staring straight ahead. He glared into faces as he passed.

The plebes recited the words in voices pitched to a yell, "And who at the worst, if he fails, at least fails while daring greatly, so that his place shall never be with those cold and timid souls who neither know victory nor defeat."

CHAPTER 10

# No Excuse, Sir!

✦

As A REWARD FOR PASSING room inspection with flying colors, Chester, Dilly, and Ranger were excused from PEP and were sent to pick up the new uniforms that would be issued to all the plebe mice in their company. The summer whites, their formal warm-weather uniforms, had been tailored to fit and were meant to be stowed with their gear until the end of Plebe Summer. This was a fine uniform made up of a white shirt, pressed trousers, a white belt with a brass buckle, and black shoulder boards. The uniform was a sign of achievement, and they all looked forward to earning the opportunity to wear it for the first time.

There was a load of new clothes to be delivered! The bundles for Sixth Company were heaped in a pile in the tailor department, and it took the nestmates many hot trips through the sultry night to get them to their wing in Bancroft Hall. On their last trip, they were intercepted by a detailer who questioned their reason for being apart from their squad. He instructed them to drop their packages and detoured them through some alleys and tunnels to help him return athletic equipment to the old gymnasium. The trio was sent back to finish their task at a run. They passed the fountain outside Dalghren Hall and eyed the cool blue water it contained. Sweat dripped off their noses and down their whiskers; their moist tails dragged behind them.

"Bath time!" Ranger yelled with his huge grin.

Shedding his exercise gear, he jumped up onto the ledge, and belly flopped into the fountain.

Dilly and Chester took a quick look around at the deserted area, whipped off their blue-rimmed T-shirts and shorts, scampered up after him, and plunged into the refreshing round pool with two quick splashes. Ranger's bold ideas always seemed to work; plus, he had a knack for staying out of trouble. They were hot and grimy, and the opportunity was handed to them like a gift.

"It's us against the Rodent!" Ranger laughed as he surfaced with a gasp.

"Gotta stay clean!" Dilly said, spitting a stream of water between his long front teeth.

Chester glanced quickly around to make sure the coast was still clear and then flipped onto his back, spreading his ears for ballast, floating for a moment. The three mice bobbed, splashed, and scrubbed underneath their furry forelegs and haunches. Ranger swam strongly across the surface and jackknifed into a dive beneath the surface, his tail pointing up like an arrow. He had been a rescue swimmer on his navy ship, he had once told them. They dunked each other a few times and then hopped down to the pavement, shaking their fur from head to tail to rid their bodies of the dripping water. It felt daring and exciting to buck the rules for those few elicit minutes. Once they had redressed, Dilly took over leading them back to the stowed bundles at a fast pace. The last of the uniform packages were scooped up and delivered to the pile, and then they ran to meet up with the other squads for formation.

Sixth Company stood rigidly at attention on the practice field. The mice had been exercising for an hour and were perspiring and limp. Chester, Dilly, and Ranger slipped quickly into position.

Fleet muttered under his breath to Dilly and Chester on either side, "You got out of a good one. We have been doing push-ups, squats, and running sprints nonstop."

The still night amplified the voice of their detailer.

It was Spleen.

The hated detailer read off a long list of duties they had to accomplish within a very short time before returning for the next training activity. Chester was making himself small in the back of the ranks, hoping to remain unnoticed.

"Camo caps, drill pretzels, whiskers trimmed, showers, teeth brushed and flossed, all ranks of military officers memorized, wash out and refill canteens…"

The plebe mice took off at a run and scurried double time up the indoor pipes to their nests. Chester had his blue book out and was shouting the ranks to Dilly and Ranger as they ran.

"Captain or Colonel, O-Six…Commander or Lieutenant Colonel, O-Five…"

Some of this was review for Ranger. Dilly and Chester had been trying to remember these for several nights. When they were tired, information seemed to skitter right out of their brains.

They burst into the nest and began going mentally down the list. They got out their trimmers, toothbrushes, and floss, wildly performing these tasks while calling out the ranks and looking at the pictures of the ribbons, pins, and bars that went along with the various officer titles. Time was running out. They found their camouflage caps and piled the pretzels by the door. Mice were pounding up and down the passageway, making for the showers or returning.

Ella scampered by with her light step, towel flapping off her waist, and shouted into their nest, "Good drip coming from the faucet on Zero Deck!"

Suddenly Dilly had a brainstorm.

"Hey, we just took a bath; check shower off the list!"

They were still even damp in a few spots! This created valuable time for the three to pour over the blue book instead of joining the crush waiting for the shower facilities. With several minutes to spare, Ranger, Dilly, and Chester were lined up back on the drill field, wearing their blue camo caps and camo shirts with their names stitched over the pocket and holding their pretzel rifles at ease, relieved to have beaten the time deadline. More and more wet mice were arriving, out of breath, scuttling into position in their squads.

Mr. Spleen stood listening. When the clock tower struck the hour, he called out, "Time!" and ordered them to attention. Four more frantic plebe mice dashed up, caps askew, banging water out of their ears with open paws, faces registering their panic. They slipped into their positions with a *whoosh*.

Now there were only five answers a plebe mouse could give for anything:

> "Yes, sir" or "yes, ma'am," "no, sir" or "no, ma'am," "no excuse, sir" or "no excuse, ma'am," "I'll find out, sir" or "I'll find out, ma'am," and "aye-aye, sir" or "aye-aye, ma'am."

There was a silence throughout the squads as they waited. Mr. Spleen stood, round eyes narrowed, tail whipping up and down at the tip. Finally he spoke.

"If you were late, raise your paw."

The four tardy rodents stoically raised their furry paws. Mr. Spleen walked up to one of them, pushing his drab-brown snout so close that their pink noses almost touched. The young plebe mouse could feel the hot breath ruffling his whiskers.

"*Why were you late?*" Mr. Spleen roared.

The mouse, being made an example of, shouted back his reply: "Sir, no excuse, sir!"

This creature had been in a long line of fellow midshipmice waiting to dash under the shower, but he could not offer that as an excuse. He could only say he was without excuse because the requirement had been to show up on time. Mr. Spleen returned to the front of the squads.

"You will all drop down and give me fifty push-ups as a thank-you to your friends who could not fulfill their duty."

The mice fell to the dusty ground and began pushing up and down counting.

"One, sir...two, sir...three, sir..." The cadence continued until all fifty had been completed.

The plebe mice stood back up to attention and waited. Again Spleen surveyed the groups in their squads. They expected to be quizzed on the ranks of officers in the military. Chester felt pretty confident that he knew them all.

"Who did not shower?"

He could feel the relaxing of the mice around him. Certainly they had all showered, hadn't they? Hadn't they? They hadn't.

Chester realized with a sick feeling in the pit of his stomach that, taken literally, he and his nestmates had not visited the showers. Slowly Dilly raised his paw and then Chester and then Ranger. The three friends stood with their forelegs up. They could have gotten away with it—no one would have known—but it was a matter of honor. They had been told to shower, and they hadn't. No one cared if they had washed a half hour before. They had been given orders, and they had skirted one of them.

The pacing detailer called them up to the front of the squads. The three stood together facing Mr. Spleen. Chester shrunk his chin into his neck, stared straight ahead, and hoped Spleen would not recognize him.

"Why didn't you three shower?" Spleen's tail was flicking angrily at the tip again.

"Sir, no excuse, sir!" they all replied.

They were not allowed to explain that they had just bathed and were squeaky clean. The question asked was had they followed all the orders explicitly, and the only answer was that they had not.

"Do you think you smell better than everyone else?"

"Sir, no, sir!" they shouted.

Chester dared not move a muscle. Suddenly the brown snout was directly in front of his face. If he had focused on the black-whiskered nose, his eyes would have crossed. He could smell Spleen's sweat.

"Mr. Chester." Tap, tap, tap went the tail. "Heard you were here. Can't believe they let you in."

Chester willed himself not to breathe. He could hear the buzzing of a large mosquito nearby.

"A troublemaker. The rules aren't meant for you, is that right?"

"Sir, no, sir!"

"No? What part of *stay out of the restricted area* did you not understand? What part of *take a shower* did you not understand?"

Chester did not have an answer. The plebe mice in the front rows who could hear Spleen's words furrowed their brows when they heard him call Chester a troublemaker. Chester, Dilly, and Ranger were never in trouble.

"You don't belong here," he spat into Chester's face. Then drawing away he raised his voice. "Your shipmates will wait for you here while you go take your showers. They will be waiting for you in the upright position at attention. I'm sure they don't mind."

The plebe mice drew themselves wearily up until they were balancing on their long hind feet, using their tails for a bit of support. They would stay like this in the hot, sultry night until Chester, Dilly, and Ranger had taken their showers, regathered their belongings, and returned. The others were to be punished for their mistake.

They had never run so hard in their lives. Panting, they quickstepped to an entrance through the stone of Bancroft Hall, skittered up the inside walls, chopped around corners, and skidded through the empty rafters.

"I never should have suggested the bath in the fountain," Ranger apologized.

"It sounded like a good idea at the time to substitute the swim for the shower," Dilly wheezed as they stampeded past their wing. "Only who would have guessed Spleen would ask us if we had actually showered?"

Chester was reasoning the situation out in his thoughtful way as he raced along, but he was only inspired to utter with a deep, tense voice, "Rat poop."

"Just run," Ranger added. "Dilly, you idiot, we would have gotten away with it if you hadn't raised your paw!"

"It was a matter of honor," Dilly replied simply.

Chester was wondering if he would have raised his paw if Dilly hadn't. Ranger said he sure wouldn't have, but he couldn't let the two of them take the blame alone.

Making sure every tuft of fur was wet, they completed the task under a dripping pipe in record time.

Sometimes it seemed that finding ways around the rigid restrictions was part of a game. This time it had not worked. They redressed rapidly and sprinted back.

The trio emerged onto the drill field at a dead run, whiskers back, out of breath, and threw themselves into position with their fellow plebe mice. Some were grunting in the dark, damp heat, hind legs shaking.

Mr. Spleen called at ease and continued shouting at the weary mice. He questioned Chester repeatedly on the rates but was unable to trip him up. Chester's stomach was in knots, and he was sweating profusely, but he willed himself to stay focused. The never-ending night wore on and on.

At last the mice were released to eat their final meal and return to their wings of Bancroft Hall. Chester's squad ate with utter exhaustion, barely having the strength to nibble on the lettuce leaves, potato peels, and barbecued chicken bits, let alone sit up straight while doing it. Across the table JP's face wore its usual inscrutable expression, but his round eyes seemed slightly glazed. Next to Chester, Bodie was learning to chew without gobbling, but he did so with unusual lethargy. He snapped to long enough to answer their detailer.

"Football practice is going fine, sir." His reply was slow and groggy.

Mr. Bravo then turned to Victor. "Victor, tell us about your day."

"A very good day, sir. I am looking forward to tomorrow," the foreign rodent replied brightly in his best American Mouse accent.

Mr. Bravo looked at him intently for a long moment. Everyone sat staring straight ahead. With a snort the detailer burst out laughing, eyes squeezed shut, long teeth exposed with genuine mirth. They all joined in with relief. Chester had never heard Mr. Bravo laugh before.

Back at their wing, Chester, Dilly, and Ranger were called to a counseling session with Mr. Bravo before the singing of "Blue and Gold" and lights-out. Bravo told the nestmates that he had heard about the punishments meted out during their midnight exercise and then allowed them to tell their side of the story. They finished by expressing remorse that their mistake had caused their ship-mates to receive the burden of extra physical effort. Mr. Bravo, an upperclassmouse and only a bit older than Chester but given authority due to his first-class, or senior-year status, listened and then shared his opinion of the episode.

"The purpose of these exercises is to train warriors who follow every order even if they don't understand the reason for it being given. Obedience is essential. Someday in a battle situation, it could mean the difference between life and death."

The three sat quietly, each concerned that they were to be given a negative report, which would affect their standing within the company.

"But you rodents give me hope! You're the whole wheel of cheese," Mr. Bravo went on with encouragement. "You stand out—you have from the beginning. You didn't have to admit your omission, but you did. You displayed the honor concept, and you care about your fellow mice. They don't blame you—at least today they don't. Previously none of you have caused problems for any of the other plebe mice; in fact, I have observed you helping the others."

Chester thought about Brown Bob and wondered if this was true.

"But rules are rules. We have them for a reason. From now on, don't look for clever ways to evade following them fully for your own personal benefit. Do I make myself clear?"

"Sir, yes, sir!" they all responded.

"Chester, Mr. Spleen had some damaging things to say about you."

Chester nodded, wondering what was coming next.

Mr. Bravo looked at him with a considering expression, his light-brown fur clean and well groomed. "I make my own opinion about rodents," Mr. Bravo finished.

The detailer rustled some papers on his desk with his neat claws, rummaging through them until he found the one he was looking for.

"Chester, these are your scores from the academic tests. You are going to skip calculations, physical properties level one, and Latin. You'll be jumping ahead of those plebe-year courses and taking some classes with the youngsters. Good job."

Dilly and Ranger peered under their eye whiskers at Chester, who avoided their gaze.

Back in their nest for lights-out, Dilly looked at Chester with mock exasperation. "You tested out of *Latin*?"

"Grandfather taught me…"

"Okay, okay." Dilly waved his paw. "But did you hear what Bravo called us?"

Energized by the praise from Mr. Bravo, Dilly stretched upright on his hind legs, one foreleg held aloft, paw curled, and snout raised so that his long front teeth were exposed.

"We're the whole wheel of cheese!" he whispered in a mock announcement. "I'm going to write that down and tack it up on the doorpost to our nest."

*If we're cheese, it must be Swiss*, Chester thought. In spite of the good news about his upcoming classes, he was still troubled about the incident with Spleen. Nothing felt *whole*; every night it seemed the detailers punched *holes* into each training experience. He was still smarting from Spleen's exposure and the price Sixth Company had to pay for their mistake.

❧

B. Wise and T. Briggs both looked through their packages sent from home that had been opened earlier in the presence of their detailer, who had sorted through them looking for items that were contraband. They had been allowed one precious phone call from home so far. On that afternoon he had stood in a room with the other plebes and had been given his phone for five minutes. They were not allowed to move as they talked, so he had stood still and listened to the familiar voices of his family, feeling proud to share his stories and a little choked up. He had told them that he was well and then lowered his voice even more and asked his mom to send some combination locks as soon as she could. He was relieved now to see there were two silver locks with black dials in his package. Now he would be able to properly lock his rifle in the gun locker. The combination locks were tucked in the box along with flavored drink powder for his water bottle, homemade chocolate-chip cookies, a large bag of salted nuts in shells, a caring note from his mom, and a funny card from his dad. Briggs had a box of crackers, his favorite whole-grain chocolate bars, and trail mix. They set them out to share with each other. A quick movement in the doorway heralded the arrival of one of the young women in their company. She popped her head in waving three pages of paper, which she held in her hand.

"I'll never have the time to read this letter! Think of all the good advice I'm missing from my dad." She sped off before Briggs and Wise could reply.

145

B. Wise thought about the brief loving words of encouragement from his parents and smiled. He appreciated everything but
couldn't dwell on it. He quickly turned his thoughts to what might
happen next. Would it ever be possible to explain this new life to
anyone who hadn't lived it? He doubted it.

Wise paused from writing his nightly paragraph and listened,
ear cocked upward.

"Hey, T, hear that? Sounds like mice scampering across our
ceiling." He cracked a peanut, chewed it rapidly, and left the rest
on his desk.

CHAPTER 11

# Mice in The Arena

⚜

THE VERY NEXT DAY, DURING the midnight meal, massive platters of peanuts in the shell were placed on every table. Chester and the other plebe mice could not believe they were being served this delicacy.

"You rodents are lucky," the detailer assigned to their squad commented with his toothy Southern drawl. "We never had goobers when I was a plebe."

Potato-chip plates heaped with chunks of oatmeal-chocolate granola clusters were also brought out and plunked down in front of the surprised midshipmice. The mice from Dietary Supply must have found a lucky stash of food.

They were always fed well because it was important that they be kept in top physical condition, and the food they were given was usually plentiful and nutritious, but this was extra special.

While the detailers were stern and pushed the plebe mice relentlessly, they also worked nonstop. They were awake before the plebe mice, retired to their nests after them, and, among their many duties, made regular visits to the storehouses below for provisions. Their job was exhausting too, though the midshipmice never thought about that. Detailers didn't complain about the long hours and physical exertion of their summer job, and the plebe mice were too busy attempting to keep up, stay on task, and stay out of trouble to give it a thought.

Bodie made particularly happy crunching noises as he chewed through a long, humped shell, eating the salty nuts with practiced speed. Ella, who loved chocolate, licked her claws daintily. The meal had a festive air even though they ate in silence. Chester watched out of the corners of his eyes as the pile of shells mounded up on the floor around them. Every so often, a dining-hall worker with a blue scarf tied over her ears rushed past with a stiff brush, pushing the shredded shells into a heap.

Before he had finished his last peanut, Bodie put out a paw. Holding the foreleg out with a clenched paw was the recognized sign for asking permission to speak.

"Go ahead, Bodie," the detailer responded.

"Please pass the peanuts."

Someone shouted, "Incoming!"

A large peanut sailed through the air like a football in the accepted manner of passing nonmessy foods. Bodie deftly caught it in his two forepaws, tucking the shell to his chest in a football hold.

The enjoyment ended as soon as they lined up and were led at a trot to the parking lot behind Dahlgren Hall. Chester's squad joined several hordes of plebe mice who were waiting quietly in ranks. Some sort of running course had been set up. Streetlights shone upon the black asphalt, reflecting off the minerals imbedded in the surface and illuminating several large objects.

Resting on the ground at the beginning of the course were two large combination locks. These were used as midshipmouse training weights. The dials were black with white numbers. The silver metal glistened under the streetlamps.

The plebe mice squatted in silence while they were given instructions.

"To compete in the heavy-weight carry, you will slip your snouts through the *U*-shaped end of the lock."

One of the detailers told them what to do as another demonstrated the procedure.

"You will hoist the whole weight, resting the flat side on your back, and carry the lock along this short mapped-out course."

Chester tried to study the locks from where he crouched. They looked formidable.

Next to the weights was a great, long log. The circumference was nearly the height of a mouse. It was a sixteen-ounce shiny wrapped pepperoni. Chester had never seen one of these in its entirety before.

The detailers began to bark instructions. "This portion of the physical challenge will require you to work together in squads, carrying the pepperoni as a team over a long, marked-out distance."

"Good gravy," Chester breathed softly to Dilly, who was at his side.

"Great Porky's ghost!" Bodie whispered to no one in particular.

The squads were told to pair up. Brown Bob immediately asked Ranger to be his partner. He had moved swiftly before anyone else. Chester looked sideways at him and felt the now familiar sting of lost respect. Victor, who was standing right beside him, clapped his paw on Chester's shoulder, requesting they work together. JP and Fleet nodded at each other, leaving Bodie with Dilly. Ella was transferred to another squad that had a single female plebe mouse.

The challenges began with the two-mouse wheelbarrow races. One mouse lay belly down while his hind feet were held up by his partner. The mouse on the ground would use his front paws, and the standing mouse would run while pushing his partner forward. On the return leg of the race, one partner was to hoist the other on his shoulders and run back.

Chester, Victor, Fleet, and JP were negotiating the positions they would take, while Dilly made it clear to Bodie that he would be doing the pushing and the lifting.

"There is no way I am going to hoist that enormous hind end!" Dilly announced emphatically, paws on his hips.

The races began. Chester's squad did well in keeping pace against the other squads. Ranger and Brown Bob were swift in the wheelbarrow leg, with Brown Bob's tough forepaws pedaling along on the ground. At the turnaround point, Ranger yanked him up to his shoulders, making excellent time on the return scramble back to the finish line. The team members were cheering modestly because the detailers were on top of them like fleas.

Next, the mice were required to lift the heavy combination lock and transfer it across a short course. Each mouse had a turn to hook the *U*-shaped end around his neck so that the flat part of the lock rested on their furry spine. One by one they staggered under the load, a detailer striding alongside yelling, "Faster, faster!" They grunted and grimaced as their backs sagged under the weight, lugging the locks inch by inch across the paced-out trail. It wasn't far, but it felt like a mile.

Chester watched as Brown Bob inserted his snout through the metal loop, gripped the yoke with his paws, and hoisted the lock onto his back with a clean jerk. Bent over, he stomped heavily along on his muscular haunches as he kept pace with the detailer, growling through gritted teeth in the night heat.

When it was Bodie's turn, the large gray-brown mouse squatted on his hind end with the lock upon his back.

"He looks like a mushroom," Dilly whispered.

*Think I'm going to bust a gut,* Chester thought.

When his name was called, Chester threaded his snout through the loop, bunched the muscles in his abdomen and thighs, squeezed his eyes shut, and lifted with all his might. The lock shifted back and forth on his narrow back until he was able to keep it balanced. He plodded, step by step, breath whistling through his two front teeth, one paw grasping the metal loop and the other poised toward the ground in case he fell, willing himself to stay upright. The muscles in his haunches were screaming—he hoped his old injury would not flare up.

The detailer next to him was hollering into his flattened golden ear, "Keep going—your granny can go faster!"

By the time he made it to the end of the course, he was trembling all over, his belly practically scraping the ground between his widespread legs.

*Not my best event,* he thought, *but I did it.*

Some mice collapsed in the field. They got up, staggered a few steps, and fell again. The detailers stood over them, forelegs flailing and screaming at them that they were leaving a shipmate in peril by giving up.

Chester watched as Ella's nestmate Shrill scuttled across the marked-out field, bent double, but keeping time with her detailer. She was quite a mouse.

After her finish she passed by him. "Piece of cheese, Cheddar."

"Chester," he said automatically.

Chester was half impressed with her strength, half annoyed at her bravado, but mostly he wished she would get his name right.

In the final race, each squad listened as they were given directions regarding the huge pepperoni. Their task was to lift and transfer the heavy pepperoni across the parking lot as a group. With their varying heights, they would have to work to keep the long sausage steady and parallel to the ground, or it would tip sideways. One misstep and the heavy weight could easily tip off balance, slipping out of their paws. This would automatically disqualify the squad *and* be a source of humiliation.

Ella was back with the squad, so they had nine plebe mice to complete the log carry. They all watched as other teams took their turns. The pepperoni carry was obviously difficult. Some groups were having trouble getting a claw hold. The shorter mice could not even be seen above the shiny plastic top. Chester's squad huddled to plan the order with which they would place themselves— who would be on the ends and who would be in the middle.

Fleet immediately began giving orders on where they should all stand. Ella rolled her eyes at the way he tried to downplay her ability.

"Why don't we put Ella in the center? We can carry the weight around her," he commented dismissively.

"I can lift as well as anybody," she said. "Better pay attention to your own ability."

"We need to stagger our heights," JP started.

"And distribute the load," Chester finished firmly in his quiet, deep voice.

"Why don't you take one end, Chester? We'll put Ranger next."

"I like that. Then you, Brown Bob, and Dilly in the center for stability, and we can all hear him call a cadence."

"Perfect. How about Victor next, then Bodie, Ella, and Fleet at the other end?"

"Let's see how that looks." Chester was thinking rapidly.

Ella grimaced at being placed next to Fleet but thought the placement sounded fair. She was more than ready to do her share.

Dilly looked at the lines of the pole and suggested grip holds. Victor and Bodie remained quiet. Victor was politely listening to

Chester, while Bodie was trying to read the ingredient list on the massive wrapper. Brown Bob paced around, anxious to get the job done. He stood next to Ranger.

"What do you think, big rodent?"

Ranger gave his trademark grin. "Like what I'm hearing from Ches, Dilly, and JP," he laughed.

Brown Bob shrugged restlessly. They spaced themselves out and looked at where their paws lined up. JP threw out more ideas.

Chester switched Bodie and Fleet, causing the white mouse to grumble. "Who put you in charge?"

Chester inwardly rolled his eyes and ignored Fleet. JP reminded everyone to use his or her tail for stability. They finally had a plan. When their squad was called, and they approached the massive sausage, Chester could see there were claw holes and rips all over the clear coating from the previous squads' attempts. They squatted down as a unit and shook out their tails.

"One, two, *three!*" the detailer called out, and the mice lifted as one.

Immediately Ella shouted with a high squeak when the meat stick began to roll forward.

"Hang on!" Her head and upper body with its distinctive ring of white fur around her neck barely showed above the pepperoni, but she yanked up with all her might.

"Lean back, lean back!" Fleet shouted. The weight was immense and difficult to hold.

"Move forward. March!" The detailer did not wait for them to steady themselves before he began to bark at them, following alongside. Dilly called out a rasping cadence as they grunted, gritted teeth, and gasped with enormous effort.

Six steps, seven steps—they were moving as one, limbs shaking from the effort of holding the pepperoni up and level. Every

one of them bore the weight, straining with each footfall. At one point a tremor went through the long pole, causing a jerking shift. They all heaved to. From down at the other end, Chester heard Bodie exhale with a muffled roar. They could not even look at each other. Either their eyes were squeezed shut in strained concentration or focused on the detailer waving them forward. Dilly kept up a singing pace, though he was wheezing with each breath. Chester's muscles were screaming, but he willed himself to keep up his end. Next to him Ranger breathed in and out with a strained "heesh...shoosh!"

Thirteen steps, fourteen steps—the mice wondered when they would be given the go-ahead to drop the log.

Ella encouraged the squad with a high cry. "Keep going!"

All were struggling to keep their claw hold; a skittering was heard here and there as one of them adjusted their grip, sweaty pads of their paws squeaking on the plastic. Chester could no longer hear the strange sound that had been emanating from Bodie's throat.

Twenty-four steps...twenty-five steps...

"Halt!"

The pepperoni crashed to the ground and rolled to a stop. Chester's squad dropped to fours, leaned onto their tails, or bent over with heaving chests. Chester's body was numb. He turned and looked down the row of his squad mates. There at the end was Bodie fallen to the ground, flat on his back...with a huge chunk of pepperoni gripped in his teeth! He had kept up his end of the pole by chomping into the sausage with his jaws. That explained the muffled roar. Ella was at his side slapping his shoulder and cheering, "Attamouse, Bodie, attamouse!"

There was confusion and difficulty in talking, as the detailers were striding about them, but it soon became clear what had happened. Fleet, who was third in from Bodie's end, had lost his grip when he tripped or slipped—no one knew. Ella had wedged herself underneath with a shoulder, while Bodie grappled the end with a mighty effort from his knees and paws, finally sinking his teeth into the top of the massive pepperoni. He continued to grip the log this way until the end of the race. The mice were spent and lay where they fell.

From the pavement somewhere nearby, Chester heard Dilly's deadpan voice call out, "Great Porky's ghost!"

For the first time, Chester's squad knew victory. They won the pepperoni log carry with the fastest time. They were exhausted and hid their excitement, but they were euphoric.

⚜

In Room 1324, B. Wise roared when he awakened the next morning and found his large bag of peanuts gaping open and empty. There was one cracked shell left on his desk but no peanuts. Across the room T. Briggs sifted through the glittering pile of granola-bar wrappers torn into minute shards next to the empty box.

"My peanuts!" yelled B. Wise.

"My granola bars!" Briggs bellowed with disgust.

"Mice," they said at the same time.

It wasn't until later that B. Wise realized his combination locks were missing too.

CHAPTER 12

# The Weak Link

❧

ALL THIRTY COMPANIES OF PLEBE mice stood arranged in their ranks, black shiny brims tilted down over steely globe eyes, staring straight ahead. Balanced on his back feet, at attention next to Chester, Fleet tucked in his white snout and whispered out of the side of his rigid mouth, "We're being taken on recon tonight."

"How do you know?" Chester whispered back.

"I overheard Spleen talking with a new detailer. We are going to have new detailers for the rest of the summer."

This was news to Chester. Could they possibly be getting rid of Spleen? But that meant Mr. Bravo would be leaving too. He would be sorry to see him go.

Fleet waited for a detailer to walk by and continued. "They are going to take us into the Rooms Below after training."

"What training?"

Chester was trying to be very quiet, but he was extremely interested in this news. Getting information ahead of time was valuable. It could give him and his squad a leg up. They rarely knew what the next moment would hold. It was a relief to have advance notice; knowing took away the stress of the perpetual question, what will happen now? He felt a little tremor of excitement. They had been waiting all summer to tour the rooms of their human

157

counterparts above and below and see how they lived! This would be their first *real* mission, and they had earned it.

"What training?" he asked Fleet again under his breath.

"I don't know," Fleet spoke after a pause, as a detailer had gone by glaring at the mice who stood with their chins tucked, faces erased into granite-hard expressions. "That's all I was able to hear."

The mice were numb from drilling with their pretzel rifles, practicing yet again for the first formal dress parade, which would mark the end of Plebe Summer. Three more weeks, or twenty-one moonrises, until the end of the rigorous training period—but that was too long to think about. They had been at it for hours, marching in precise formation with the pretzels over their right shoulders in the nighttime heat. Bodie later said he did not think he would ever be able to eat a pretzel again.

"I'll believe that when I see it," Dilly remarked with a snort.

The plebe mice were dressed in their white alphas—the midshipmouse covers with the black brim and high white crown snug between their ears and black kerchiefs knotted around the neck of their blouses. Soon they would be issued their fine midshipmouse summer white uniform.

Within an hour the mice were escorted to their crawl space auditorium for the training brief. A uniformed mouse introduced as Captain Field strode to the edge of the stage to deliver the information. At this point the rumor had spread by word-of-mouse, and everyone knew they were being prepared to venture into the Rooms Above and Below. The excitement in the brief area was intense. Reconnaissance, or "recon," involved exploring far into Bancroft Hall in search of supplies, and the young midshipmice were more than ready.

On a wall at the end of the briefing room was a diagram of some sort of mechanism that Chester couldn't make out. The picture showed a flat, rectangular board labeled as "wood" with a spring and bars labeled as "metal" attached to the top. There was also a side view and a top view of the apparatus. In the side view, an arrow arced across the apparatus to show how a metal piece sprung from one position to another. It looked as if there were a chunk of cheese poised at one end. They all looked at the diagram curiously.

"This is what our brothers-in-arms use to deter marauders, foreign and domestic, from entering their perimeters." Captain Field held a long stick to point at the diagram.

"What kind of marauders?" Dilly breathed to Ranger.

"Beats me. Maybe rats or cats or something. Saw these on a ship one time. Knew to stay clear," he answered out of the corner of his snout.

"They are also called mouse traps," JP said flatly from behind.

*What?* Chester thought. *Mouse traps?* The room whirled for a moment, and then he remembered Grandfather's warning that not all mice were trustworthy or out for the common good. These traps must be deterrents for those sorts. That made him feel better.

Captain Field continued to describe the marauder traps, or MTs, which they were commonly called at the Naval Mouse Academy.

"Be careful of these weapons. Do not go near them. Sometimes cheese is used as bait and sometimes peanut butter. It is very enticing to the enemy. We have nothing to do with these. Examine the drawing carefully, and memorize it. In the wrong hands, these weapons are deadly to you."

Their instructor looked over his glasses at the serious rodents. His face was grave. The plebe mice glanced around at each other. They had not expected to encounter danger so soon.

"If you are cautious and vigilant," Captain Field continued, "you have no reason to fear. We go on recon for a reason—to get our supplies and to maintain stability with our human compatriots as we fortify the bastion together. Is that clear?"

"Sir, yes, sir!" they bellowed back.

"Your detailers will lead you on your first mission into the interior this very night. Follow their examples and instructions to the letter. You will be bringing in new parade rifles and gathering cloth for your service dress blues, which are your winter formal uniforms."

Chester knew exactly what uniform Captain Field was describing. He could picture Grandfather in his old dark suit jacket and pants, the deep-hued cloth, which was really more black than blue, gold stripes on the sleeves, and a double row of brass buttons—only the sleeves of *their* issued coats would be bare of stripes because they were still plebes. The midshipmice would earn a stripe or other marking each season as they progressed from plebe to youngster to second class and finally to first class, like their detailers.

"Your cold-weather, special occasion uniforms will be made from these materials," Captain Field continued. "This is a supply run. Your detailers may have other items that they will tell you to obtain. Handle this well, and you move on. Fail, and your eligibility as a USNMA midshipmouse is questionable. Am I making myself clear?"

"Sir, yes, sir!" they shouted again.

"Full speed ahead!" the instructor barked, leaning forward on his long hind feet, front teeth glinting, as he dismissed them into the charge of their detailers.

The squads lined up in the throughway outside a row of nests, awaiting assignment into groups. They were often teamed with mice from other squads to promote adaptability. The mice were surprised that they were not being required to wear any of their camouflage gear but soon learned that they melded into the darkness better in their natural fur—which maybe was not true for Fleet, but what was good for one was good for all. Their blue camo shirts with matching caps were really for water missions. The goal was for them to slip in and slip out in the dark without waking their human friends.

Chester found himself placed with three mice from another squad and a detailer he had never met before. He was relieved that Mr. Spleen's duty was over for the rest of the summer. He could breathe easier now. It would be a tremendous relief not to have to watch out for Spleen and worry about the trouble he might make for him. He didn't care if he never saw that sweaty, angry mouse again.

The mice stood in their clusters, awaiting the next command. Chester looked at the three other rodents he would be reconnoitering with: a caramel-colored female with dark eyelashes and long, dark whiskers named Lani; Godfrey, who played in drum and bugle; and Lester, a pale mouse with patchy fur. They all nodded, ears perked, and swiveled forward, awaiting orders. Chester could not help but notice that Lester was twitchy. He shuffled and kept his triangle-shaped head low after the introduction, glancing side to side. His tail was limp and listless.

Chester raised a brow at Godfrey. "Is he okay?" he whispered.

"Not doing too well this summer," the pleasant-voiced mouse quietly answered. "He's my nestmate. The brief on marauder traps might have been the last straw."

Godfrey turned on his hind feet and gave Lester's furry shoulder a clap with his big paw. Chester watched their interchange. Lester responded to the encouraging touch by standing still, shaking his snout, and then shrugging off the paw. Godfrey turned, sighed, and rolled his eyes skyward.

"I'm trying," the patient mouse mouthed.

Chester knew without being told that Lester was a weak link. He felt bad for the mouse, who appeared to be shrinking under the immense pressure of Plebe Summer, but he wondered how it would affect their mission. He felt the need to try to shore him up, but before he could say anything, they were called to attention.

The commanding mouse from the briefing, Captain Field, strode down along the bulkhead on all fours, looking from side to side at the lines of mice who had immediately pulled to attention. He called out words of old as he quickly moved through the ranks: "Sail fast…sail fast…sail fast!"

Chester felt a frisson of excitement and challenge. He was ready to support the mission.

Chester's detailer pulled off his yellow shirt and tucked it away in a corner. The detailers were using natural camouflage to make themselves indistinguishable from their environment. Chester looked down the long hallway of plebe mice gathered around the older first-class midshipmice. He thought he could just see Brown Bob's distinctive shiny coat near Ranger. The pang of losing his respect nagged at Chester again. Whose team would he be on? Would *their* mission be a success? He looked for Dilly and could not find him in the throng of four-legged bodies. He turned his attention resolutely back to the detailer standing before him. Mr. Cliff was his name, and he spoke in a clipped fashion, slapping the tip of his tail with each point.

"All right, you four, here is our mission. We are going on recon in another wing of Bancroft Hall. All the teams are being spread out, and we've got a long way to go. Once we get to our destination, we slip in without noise, and we leave in the same manner. We do not utter a sound: no squeaking or exaggerated gnawing. We bring out what we need, and we leave nothing behind. Nothing. Is that clear? We are not to disturb the warriors who live among us, who carry the burden of the daytime watch."

The four plebe mice stood with their backs against a wall. Chester heard the echo of the others' affirmative "Sir, yes, sir!"

"We will go in formation. I lead, and you follow. I am not watching to see if you can keep up with me. Either you do, or you don't. If you fall behind, find the way back by yourself. But I wouldn't consider that an option if I were you."

Mr. Cliff stared down his long, pointy nose under his lowered whiskery brow for a long minute. Chester thought he could hear a dry swallow from Lester.

"There will be no need to talk until we get to the tunnel that takes us into the room. I will give you your final instructions then. Any questions?"

"Sir, no, sir!"

He turned and gestured for Lani to fall in behind him, followed by Lester and then Godfrey. Chester would take up the rear.

Heading out at a trot, Mr. Cliff set the pace through the rafters of the ceiling. After many twists and turns, the small recon unit came to the end of the passage and lined up at a hole that had been chewed through the wall around a wire. One at a time, they grabbed the black plastic-coated wire and slid down to the next level. At the bottom their detailer led them through a small chink in the wall board and onto a shiny gray floor. Keeping close to the corridor walls, they began running along what seemed like miles of hallway. At any doorway with a light, they stopped and waited for Mr. Cliff to give the all clear before they shot across the open area to the gleaming passage beyond. The corridor ended at a stairwell, and their detailer squeezed through a narrow opening about the width of an Oreo turned on its side.

Around the time they hit the stairwell, Chester noticed Lester was slowing down. Godfrey gave him a quick word of encouragement and shoved him with his paw when he started to back up out of the tiny gap in the wall. On the other side, Mr. Cliff called them to a halt. They were all breathing hard. The route had been so long that Chester did not think he could get back on his own. He had given up memorizing after the tenth or twelfth twist and turn.

"We are right outside our object," Cliff mouthed quietly. "I was scouting yesterday, and they have our supply. Chester, you are going to secure drill rifles. These can be found in the lockers. Lani, we will need rope to bring back the rifles. Find it wherever you can. Lester, you are to look for the black cloth and obtain a sizable amount. Godfrey, you stand watch in the room while I assist your shipmates."

Godfrey was disappointed not to be rooting among the cabinets, but he would do as he was ordered. Mr. Cliff pushed through a hole, followed energetically by Lani, who slipped through with a whip of her slender tail. Outside the opening, Lester began to back up again.

"I'm not going in there!" he whispered furiously.

Chester was taken aback but tried to encourage him.

"We're all going in. We'll get our things and leave. It'll be fast."

"If we go in, we may not come back out! What about those marauder…?"

Lester was starting to sound slightly hysterical, but Godfrey interrupted him. "Are you worried about the MTs? Because if you are—"

"Marauder traps! What about the marauders?" Lester hissed. "We don't even know who's in here!" His wild eyes began to dart around.

Godfrey took Lester's foreleg to lead him toward the crevice.

Lester shook it off angrily. "Don't touch me!" His voice was starting to grow shrill, mottled hair standing on end, his tail rasping back and forth across the board behind him.

Chester looked at Godfrey and then calmly beckoned to Lester, "Come on, just follow me." Was he nuts even to be saying this?

Godfrey encouraged Lester with a low, calm voice. "First Chester will go, then you, and I will be right behind."

Lester's glance darted at both of them like a caged rat. "I told you—I'm not going *in*!"

Chester finally shrugged. He squeezed through the opening and found himself in an enclosed space, squirming and pushing around boxes and bags.

After a moment Godfrey's shape emerged next to him. "I've never seen him like this," he whispered into Chester's cupped ear.

Mr. Cliff peered at the two in the dark and mouthed, "Where is Lester?"

Neither of the two mice answered. They stood silently.

Mr. Cliff uttered an oath and gripped Godfrey by the shoulder. "You're in charge of obtaining cloth, plebe mouse."

Their detailer indicated where to find the required items, pointing with his muscular paw tipped with strong nails. Soon Lani had found her supply and was busily chewing through black ropes with plastic ends, which were laced through shiny black shoes. Godfrey had pulled himself up a long strip of material and was gnawing efficiently through the length, allowing the black cloth pieces to drop to the ground. Mr. Cliff led Chester underneath a door of the small, cramped space and into the main part of the room. On three sides were desks and chairs, topped way up high by three narrow bunks. On each bed, snoring or breathing heavily, were their brothers-in-arms. Real humans. Midshipmen. Chester was in awe.

Next to the closet, where Lani and Godfrey worked busily, was a locker, which was slightly ajar. Mr. Cliff pointed a claw to the opening and gestured for Chester to find a way in. Chester climbed up a chair leg, leaped from the seat to the desk, and assessed the situation. The first locker next to the desk had a gleaming lock looped through a clasp. It was one of their training weights! He skirted over the top of this secured closet and shimmied into the second locker. It was a treasure trove of food! Boxes of cookies, packages of crackers, and blocks of wrapped whole-grain fig bars were stacked here and there. He rummaged through the collection, disciplining himself not to sample even a crumb. After sorting and sniffing a bit more, he found several small cardboard boxes covered in cellophane, which contained pretzel sticks. Pay dirt! He quickly slit open the clear top with his razor-sharp teeth and began unloading the salty sticks. At the opening to the locker, he looked down to the polished gray floor and signaled to his detailer.

Mr. Cliff indicated Chester should begin dropping the sticks one by one, and he would catch them. Soon Lani joined them with four lengths of rope, one end chewed and the other coated with hard plastic. She helped catch the drill rifle pretzels before they hit the ground and shattered. Godfrey emerged from the closet, four pieces of cloth bundled into a wad, pushing them with his snout. Cliff motioned for them to strap the sticks to each other's backs by wrapping the ropes around their furry middles. Each took a piece of cloth in his or her teeth. Mr. Cliff took Lester's load upon his own back.

Chester, Lani, and Godfrey looked about the neat room curiously. They had not seen any marauder traps or marauders! The lumps on the beds, draped loosely with sheets, breathed heavily, and once one of the humans moved in his sleep, but there was nothing more frightening than that. The three plebe mice were euphoric. They followed Mr. Cliff back through the closet and into the crawl space behind the room. There they found Lester in a miserable heap crammed in a corner. Mr. Cliff did not speak to him, nor did he transfer the load of pretzels from his back to Lester's. The plebe mice followed their detailer, silently, back the way they had come.

After unloading the supplies with precision, the mice were released to their nests. Chester watched Mr. Cliff speak quietly to Lester and lead him away. He could only imagine what was going to happen, and it wouldn't be good. Lester would probably be separated and sent home. Chester felt sorry for the mouse, but he knew he would never want to be paired with him on a mission again. Lester was unsafe.

All the mice were bursting to tell their shipmates their stories, and soon there was jubilation up and down the throughway. High fives and squeaks of triumph abounded as they shared tales of their first reconnaissance into the Rooms Above and Below. They knew it was a test of their courage, efficiency, and ability to take orders and carry them out in an alert, military manner.

Dilly came bursting through the entrance to their nest. "Who's the Rodent?"

Ranger had just been regaling Chester with the tale of his recon run. He had been with Brown Bob and a plebe mouse from Fifth Company named James. Their task had been to restock the detailers' yellow shirts. They had found the fabric draped over the back of a chair in their target room, but—*phew*—had it smelled!

James had comically pantomimed passing out in front of their detailer, who miraculously had snickered quietly. Their sensitive noses had rebelled at being so close to the odor, but they had muscled through and even managed to drag the whole bundle back without having to gnaw off pieces. That had been Brown Bob's idea. At his name, Brown Bob, who was passing by in the passageway, stuck his glossy brown snout into their nest and gave Ranger a thumbs-up. Ranger hollered a good-natured "Get outa here!" grinning widely.

Dilly was dancing with excitement. His team had encountered a marauder trap. Just as they had been informed, it had held a blob of peanut butter and was huge! Chester wanted to know what it looked like up close, while Ranger sat back nodding knowledgeably.

"Those things are massive!" Dilly said, embellishing his story, eyes glittering with life.

Then he shared what happened when they inspected the MT from a safe distance. It turned out that the trap had a name inscribed in great blocky orange letters across the wooden board— Victor. Victor, who was in Dilly's group, had been shocked and saddened.

"That is my name! Someone wishes to trap me and make me go pfffft? They do not know me. Why do they single me out?"

The detailer in Dilly's group reassured Victor that it had nothing to do with him. "They all say that. I think it's the name of the human who made them."

Victor was only slightly appeased and took to looking over his shoulder.

Chester told his story and ended with the outcome of Lester's refusal to obey.

"Mr. Cliff led him away after we were dismissed. He's definitely going Tango."

Chester knew that Godfrey was soon going to be without a roommate, and either Lester would leave voluntarily or would be separated from the military via an official chain of command. In any case he would be placed in Tango Company until a decision could be made. It was an odd feeling to think that of one of their ranks would be leaving. They had all worked so hard for so long. How could any mouse give up now, especially since they were half-way through Plebe Summer? But Lester had definitely been a weak link.

⚜

B. Wise glanced around the room, forgetting again that there was no clock. Even the hallway clocks were covered with boxes so that the plebes would never know the time. They were to be kept in the dark about everything, including the passage of time, adding to their dependence on their detailers. He turned back to his immediate problem.

"We're going to have to get traps, Briggs. We had mice again last night."

"I thought you had your food in plastic boxes."

"Not everything. I had some extra snacks lying around. Utter destruction."

"Well, we were lucky. I heard some plebes had uniforms chewed up, and one of the detailers is missing his shirt. Think it's a prank?"

"Only if the detailers did it, and they haven't been acting too humorous. Anyway, all I know is we had mice in *our* room last night. Do you think the Midshipman Store sells mousetraps?"

"No clue. I don't even know if we are going to be escorted there to shop for personal supplies again before the end of Plebe

170

Summer. In any case I don't want a squashed, stinking rodent in our room. Can't we do something else?"

"I'll come up with a plan," B. Wise promised. "I've had it with these pests. Believe me, this is war!"

CHAPTER 13

# A Bright Moment

❖

CHESTER HAD NEVER BEEN IN such fine physical shape in his life. His round, furry tummy had flattened, and his short front legs and wide haunches had thickened with muscles. Not only that, his head felt positively *stuffed* with professional knowledge.

He sat at his study area in the nest, blue book in front of his tawny nose, gnawing through a tasty piece of beef jerky. Dilly crunched on a large crispy puff of caramel corn, both of which had arrived in a package from Chester's mama. The paper-wrapped bundle had been delivered the night before via Mouse Mail. It had been well secured to keep out any pests. The plebe mice were cautioned to store their snacks from home in well-wrapped bundles because ants could be a pesky problem. He had warned Mama about this in his second letter home, and she had done her best. It was triple wrapped in newspaper and wound tight with string.

Chester placed a large glistening piece of popcorn on Ranger's desk, awaiting his return from high-dive practice. Ranger's amazing collection of sugary treats had grown enormous, yet his teeth remained strong and pearly white.

Dilly hummed marching and running cadences while he chewed. Chester soon found himself inserting the words following each hummed musical refrain.

"We jogged nine miles, and we ran three…"

172

Dilly hummed again, and Chester spoke the chant through his rapid chewing.

"The chief was yelling, 'Follow me!'"

They were both bobbing their triangular heads side to side, eyes shut, with mutual enjoyment as they ate the tasty snacks. Rarely were they left alone for any length of time, and Dilly and Chester were taking advantage of it. Dilly hummed again, and Chester began to make up silly words.

"Dilly's got a pinky ear..." The humming continued louder. "And he's got a stinky—"

"Hey!" Dilly interjected. "Knock it off! You sing, and I'll make up the words."

Chester cleared his throat with a low chuckle and began a thrum of noise to the tune of "Strings and Strands and Rubber Bands." They both laughed.

"Try again!" said Dilly.

Chester complied with a deep-voiced hum of their marching cadence, which was woefully off-key. Grandfather had often said, "That mouse has a tin ear!" but Chester liked to sing anyway.

Dilly bit off another mouthful of airy sweet, munching with thought, his short blond whiskers wagging. It was difficult for Chester to hum music while chewing the thick dried meat, but they were having so much fun, it didn't matter. He hummed along in a low rumble, waiting for Dilly to make up new words.

"We're the three for history...Ranger, Chester, Dilleeeeee...it does not matter where we end...we'll always defend the bastion!"

"One, two..." Chester intoned deeply.

"Attention on deck!" Dilly yelled and leaped to his hind legs.

Chester scrambled up after him.

A blue-uniformed officer stood in the entrance of the nest accompanied by two detailers. Chester quickly looked at the officer's insignias to identify his rank.

Just the night before he had been walking the straight paths of the Yard with two other mice from his company as they scurried with quick steps to their destination. They had been on their way to the sailing center for small-boat-sailing practice. As they talked quietly, their eyes roved constantly, on the lookout for senior officers. Failure to recognize a mouse of rank was fatal. It was just as bad to wrongly salute an enlisted mouse. Chiefs were particularly sticky about this. They were the highest rank in the navy without being officers, and they would chew you up and spit you out the side of their snout if you saluted them. Across the grass Chester had seen a gray mouse with brass and bars.

"What service…do we salute?" the plebe mouse next to him had begun to mutter the question. They were all squinting and peering at the uniform. "Do we? *Do we?*"

The sturdy mouse approached in his dark-green uniform with gold insignia.

"Yes!" Chester hissed, and the three mice stood tall, snapping their paws in an angled salute.

"Good evening, sir!" they had chorused.

The officer mouse had saluted back, nodding his whiskers in reply, and released them from their salute by lowering his paw first.

Chester now looked at this senior mouse in a marine uniform standing in their nest, recognizing his rank from all the studying they had done.

"This is Major General Growler," one of the detailers informed them. "He asked to be given a tour of Bancroft Hall."

"At ease, rodents," the major general said, but Dilly and Chester barely relaxed a muscle.

"I used to live in this nest!" The officer was sniffing around the room, investigating corners and peering into lockers with a "May I?"

"Such great memories!" he boomed. "How is the summer going, fellas?"

Chester and Dilly both replied affirmatively and positively. Neither was going to say what they really thought: "Exhausting, stressful. I'm tired of getting yelled at!"

But, Chester thought as he stared straight ahead at a spot just above the major general's shoulder, though every night was a challenge, there had been gratification in small victories. The previous silly singing with Dilly had been a bright spot, as had been other moments with Ranger and the new friends in their squad. He looked forward to the end of Plebe Summer because there would be a slight lessening of pressure and a change in the training, but he also recognized that the friendships being formed under the strain of Plebe Summer were irreplaceable. Those bonds were strengthening and would help them through their four seasons at the Naval Mouse Academy.

"What is next on your agenda?" the major general continued his questioning.

Neither Dilly nor Chester could respond because they did not know.

The detailers escorted the major general out of the nest but not before Chester and Dilly overheard one of them answer his question.

"Company Fisticuff Competition begins tonight, sir."

"Ah, the Fisticuff Smoker! Good times!" the major general boomed.

Chester and Dilly looked at each other. Fun over.

⚜

B. Wise stood before the mirror in their quarters dressed in white works alpha: a sailor blouse with a white T-shirt just visible underneath his tunic, black neckerchief, and white drawstring pants. He tried on the midshipmen's cover, pulling the black brim low over his eyes. T. Briggs rushed around the room, undoing the lock on his cupboard, and removed his heavy drill rifle. B. Wise stepped quickly to his own closet to unclasp the bike chain that dangled there in order to remove his rifle for parade practice.

"I sure would like to know what happened to my combination locks!" he exclaimed to his roommate. "If someone fesses up and returns them, I'll give you your bike lock back."

"I hope they do. I'm down to one combination lock myself. The Lock Monster still has my other one. Any sign of mice last night?" Briggs asked as he ran a toothbrush over his teeth while holding up the menu for the day in front of his face.

"Nope, but I came up with a plan. I've got a foolproof mouse trap in mind. Read the menu out loud, Briggsy!"

## CHAPTER 14

# Redemption of Sorts

❧

THE PLEBE MICE FROM SIXTH Company squatted in rows on the gymnasium floor. All across the polished wooden slats, mice from the different companies were being matched up for the Fisticuff Competition, or Smoker, as it was called. Not everyone would spar; it was up to the detailers to decide which rodents in each company would face off. The winners from each of the thirty companies would be entered into the final tournament. A fierce rivalry existed among the companies. They had been competing all summer to see who would be the best. It was not just the competitive spirit of Plebe Summer; they were vying for the honor of being named the Color Company, the company of mice that had earned the most overall points in athletics, professional knowledge, and military precision. The winning company would be announced at the end of Plebe Summer.

Chester squatted next to JP and Ella.

Ella whispered, "I know I won't be selected to fight—it's not my strength—but by Gouda, I would like to try!" She pounded her clenched paw on the wooden floor.

Chester was pretty sure he would not be chosen either. He had grown stronger, but he was not as skilled a fighter as Ranger or Brown Bob—certainly not in a league with Brown Bob, who was on the fisticuff team. These were quick matches: one round and the detailers called the winner. The plebe mice were restless, adrenaline pumping, talking quietly among themselves.

The detailers began announcing pairs from Sixth Company. The first match was between JP and a two-tone mouse from another squad. They were fitted with spongy headgear to protect their sensitive ears and given instructions. They faced off, paws up and clenched. This was bare-knuckle fighting. The mice threw punches and body blocks and swung their hind legs. Only tails were off-limits. Within a short time, it became clear that JP was the better fighter, and he was soon declared the winner.

Across the room shouts rang out as the plebe mice rooted for their favorites. Chester saw Ranger called up to meet a tall deep-gray field mouse who was a skilled swimmer. He cheered when Ranger dispatched his opponent quickly. Over to his right, he saw a bout begin between Godfrey and a stocky beige rodent. Godfrey was an elegant fighter, nimble on his feet. It was a close match. Godfrey was long and selective with his jabs; his opponent was short and rough but powerful. In the end the stocky rodent won, but everyone cheered for Godfrey's good effort.

The din in the room was growing. Chester thought he could not be hearing correctly when it sounded as though his name was called.

Brown Bob unfolded himself from the floor and entered the match area.

"What?" Chester was saying to those around him.

"It's you and Brown Bob!" Ella patted his front leg with what looked like alarm or pity.

Dilly, who was behind him, swatted him on the back encouragingly. "You can do it, Ches. Show him what you've got!"

He didn't sound very confident.

He heard Shrill call out, "Brown Bob against Chunky!"

Chester's head was swimming. He didn't stand a chance.

They both were fitted with the protective headgear and squared off. Chester quickly decided he was going to throw everything he had at Brown Bob and get out of there quickly. He just hoped he would perform well enough to walk away with his head up and with the least amount of damage inflicted to his body and reputation. Brown Bob immediately put his forehead down and began to move efficiently on his narrow feet. Chester felt his whole body tense. He squinted his eyes and shot punches wildly, forelegs flailing, connecting with very few. A whirlwind of action, his hind legs were kicking the air. Brown Bob hunched his powerful shoulders, and suddenly everything happened at once. The fur was a blur between the two of them for the briefest of moments, and then somehow Brown Bob pitched to his knees, blood squirting from his snout. No one could say exactly how it happened.

The detailers stopped the match, and Chester was declared the winner. One of the yellow-shirted mice brought a cloth over to staunch the flow from Brown Bob's face. A piece of gauze was called for and tied in a knot around his pointy snout. Though he tried to wave the detailer off, Brown Bob was led away.

Chester was in a daze. He had beat Brown Bob! His squad mates were cheering wildly. Many mice had expected Brown Bob to take the whole tournament, and now he was out in the first round! Chester sat down. Dilly leaned forward, clapping him on the back.

"I won." Chester was still in a state of disbelief.

"Holey Swiss cheese, it wasn't very pretty. You were a wild mouse out there, but you did it!"

The matches were continuing all around as opponents vied for a chance to earn the right to represent their company. Ranger had been placed against a tough buff-colored mouse from the football team and once again came out ahead in the round. JP was battling hard against Pedro, who was a popular rodent. It was a very close call, but JP was declared the winner.

Chester quickly realized that he would have to enter the ring again. He did not have long to wait. He was called up to fight against Primo, one of the mice on the fisticuff team. *Good Gravy*, he thought.

"Do it again! Do it again!" Ella, Dilly, and Victor had begun a chant.

Chester heard Godfrey and Lani join in. Only Bodie and Fleet were silent. Bodie looked distracted, and Fleet was probably annoyed he had not been called up to box. Chester donned the rubber head covering and took a deep breath, trying to concentrate. He knew in his heart that his win over Brown Bob had been a fluke.

"Do it again! Do it again!"

He gave it his all, but he was no match for Primo. He got in a few hits, but he was mainly concerned with self-preservation. Primo was a real fighter, using skill and strength to keep the upper paw throughout the match. Primo won efficiently and swiftly.

Chester passed Mr. Cliff, the new detailer who had led him on recon.

The older mouse gave him a nod of respect. "Good try, plebe. He's a tough fighter. Amazing knockdown of Brown Bob!"

Chester didn't know if he was glad or sorry that it was all over. *Glad.*

Primo was next called to take on JP. Across the floor Chester saw the amber glint of Ranger's fur in a clinch against the stocky rodent who had defeated Godfrey. They were fighting hard. He looked back to see the short dove-gray fur on JP's back bunched over his muscles as he steadily and methodically tried to keep up with Primo.

Chester's squad was screaming for JP and Ranger. Turning their furry heads from one direction to the other, they applauded and shouted their encouragement.

JP began to flag, while Primo's skills took over. The match ended with Primo taking the win. A moment later Ranger landed the last punch on the stocky rodent, and his front leg was raised by the detailer monitoring the round.

After the preliminary rounds, it was decided Primo and Ranger would fight each other to represent Sixth Company.

All the mice gathered around to watch the final battle. Both contenders were popular mice. Ranger threw back his snout and widened his grin as the two bumped clenched paws to begin the match. Primo responded with a smirk and a nod. The shouts were deafening as the two large mice began to jab and throw kicks. They were evenly matched; when one got in a good punch, the other followed with an equally good return. Primo threw a side blow from his powerful left back haunch, which caused Ranger to stagger for a moment. His squad responded with squeaks and shrieks of encouragement.

"Get back in there, Ranger! Give it to him!"

Primo's friends were equally loud.

"You've got him, Primo! Finish him off!"

Ranger swung his right back foot powerfully, but it glanced off Primo's flank as he moved quickly away. Primo landed a punch on Ranger's shoulder. Chester's squad groaned. That was his dominant joint for his right foreleg. Primo blocked another kick and then leaned in for the kill when Ranger threw himself sideways and swung his haunches into an arcing body blow. The force struck Primo off his balance and pitched him into a spin off his left heel.

He teetered for a moment and then crashed to the ground. The plebe mice exploded into wild cheers and some boos. Mr. Cliff called the match. Ranger stood with his paw held up in the air, the winner of the Sixth Company Fisticuff Competition.

Every mouse in their wing had been congratulating Ranger once they were in Bancroft Hall changing for their midnight meal. Ranger was humble in his victory, giving much credit to Primo's skills. Many even stopped to slap Chester on the back, expressing admiration for his first-round knockdown of Brown Bob. He felt like somewhat of a hero, though the praise was not sitting easily on his shoulders.

In their nest as they slipped quickly into their white works, readying for formation before the meal, Dilly and Chester asked Ranger where he had learned the last move that had clinched the fight for him.

"This evening before the fights began, I asked Brown Bob to show me a good move. That was the one he taught me."

Chester and Dilly were awestruck.

"You learned that move tonight?" Dilly asked.

"Yeah. When we were in the stairwell. Mr. Cliff was around the corner, so he didn't see."

His nestmates just shook their head at his amazing confidence.

"Chester! What was the move you used to take down Brown Bob?" Ranger asked.

"I'm not really sure. I think it was an accident. I was moving to protect myself, and the next thing I knew he was on the floor. Does anyone know how he is?"

"Bodie told me he has a broken snout. He's SIQ until tomorrow," Ranger informed him.

Brown Bob would be confined to his nest, sick in quarters, unable to leave.

Throughout the midnight meal and the training exercises that followed, Chester continued to think about the fight. He felt awful about Brown Bob's injury. He wanted to say something to him, but he didn't know what that might be. He had not really talked to him since the debacle with the sponge boat.

After the singing of "Blue and Gold," Chester couldn't wait any longer. He rushed around with Dilly and Ranger to get ready for an upcoming inspection and then crept down to Bodie and Brown Bob's nest. It was late. Brown Bob lay in his rack, a splint on his snout tied with a white strip of cloth. On top, a wrapped ice chip rested between his eyes.

"Hey, Brown Bob." Chester stood quietly by the silent mouse, who did not answer. "How you feeling?" he finally asked.

"Like a million cheese crackers," the injured mouse replied.

A silence stretched on. Chester tried again.

"You know that move you taught Ranger? It helped him win his match."

"That's great. Heard he won the tournament." Brown Bob didn't actually sound that happy about it.

"Yeah...you know I lost my next match after you." Chester was relieved to be able to talk about it.

"I wish you'd won."

"You do?"

"Yeah, then I wouldn't look so bad after my loss to you."

Chester couldn't tell if Brown Bob was joking or not.

"About that...you were going to beat me. Mine was a lucky blow. I was really trying to defend myself. When you leaned in, I brought up my leg to protect my belly. Somehow my knee and your snout connected. Sorry."

Brown Bob took the ice off his face and looked at Chester for the first time.

"I know, Chester. I can't believe I did that. It was amateur."

Now Chester realized what was really eating at Brown Bob. He had lost, he had been beaten by an inferior opponent, and he had made a mistake. And to top it all off, he had a broken snout. Fleet was often irritable because he wanted to win. Brown Bob was mad because he *expected* to win.

"Sorry about your snout," Chester offered, starting to feel a little annoyed that Brown Bob was not being very gracious about accepting his apology.

Just then Bodie entered the nest, carrying another chunk of ice.

"Hey, Chester! I hear your name is being put in for a commendation for breaking Bob's snout! The paper is being sent up the chain of command."

The injured mouse threw his head back with a muffled snort and eased the ice back onto the sore spot.

Chester stood awkwardly, staring at Bodie's amazed face. Before he left the room, he gave a last attempt to set things right with Brown Bob.

"You're an excellent bare-knuckle boxer, Brown Bob...everyone knows that."

There was no reply from underneath the cold pack. Chester stepped quietly out.

❧

At the end of the day, B. Wise and T. Briggs wrote their required paragraphs, which were to contain thoughts about themselves and their training. The plebes did this every night.

"Think they're trying to make sure we're still sane?" Briggs asked. "What are you writing about tonight?"

"I want the detailers to know that I'm doing my best to find combination locks and that I'm mad my new ones are missing. I'm also saying that I have figured out a way to combat the mice. That will show whoever reads these that I'm still in the game!"

Before lights-out, B. Wise showed T. Briggs the elaborate trap he had devised to capture the invading mice. Next to his desk chair, he had placed his tall, rectangular trash can. A twelve-inch ruler was laid from the chair seat across to the edge of the can. One end just barely rested on the chair and was balanced at the end over-hanging the can with a large chunk of orange cheese. It was a very smelly, ripe piece of cheese. B. Wise walked his fingers along the ruler to mimic the motion of a mouse moving from the chair to the cheese. When the weight of his fingers reached a certain point along the ruler, the whole apparatus tipped and plunged into the bottom of the receptacle.

"Brilliant, B," breathed T. Briggs.

CHAPTER 15

# Mouse Down

❧

IF THE PLEBE MICE THOUGHT that the second half of Plebe Summer was going to be made easier by the new detailers, that idea was dispelled when they met Miss Chèvre.

In some ways the plebe mice felt as though they were starting all over. But one thing remained unchanged: these unfamiliar upperclassmice, like their old detailers, continued to make it their daily business to work them hard from sundown to sunup.

Chester certainly did not miss Spleen, but he did miss the familiarity of the first set of detailers. And they all missed Mr. Bravo.

*At least I had learned what to expect*, he thought.

One night when they were escorted back to Bancroft Hall after close-order drill marching practice, they dispersed to return their pretzel rifles to their quarters.

Dilly commented under his breath as they trotted along at a good clip, "Now we have to prove ourselves all over again."

"Do you feel like you have? I'm not sure I've proven myself yet," Ella replied.

"That's not all bad," Chester assured her. "I've been doing my best not to be noticed!"

"That worked fine until the Fisticuff Smoker." Dilly's voice was dry.

"Yes." Chester was silent, but a small smile curved his snout.

Some of the plebe mice said that the second-set detailers were supposed to build them back up after being torn down by the first-set detailers of Plebe Summer. Chester thought they were still doing a fine job of wearing them down.

It was Miss Chèvre who was making life particularly difficult, not because of overly tough expectations but because *no one* could pronounce her name. Miss Chèvre had been named after her mother's favorite French cheese, which was nice for her but ridiculous for anyone trying to say it the proper way. She was perfectly fair unless one of the plebe mice mispronounced Chèvre, which was most of the time. Chester and his shipmates figured out they were safe when only a "Ma'am, yes, ma'am" was required, but often other detailers would put them in a position to have to speak her name. They laughed as they watched the plebe mice squirm, trying to muddle through the tough pronunciation, and snickered when Miss Chèvre flipped her slender snout in the air when the plebe mice got it wrong.

On the second evening after her arrival, Chester's squad was grouped in a semicircle, receiving instruction. Miss Chèvre approached and stood expectantly.

"Good evening, Miss..." The chorus of voices petered out into faint mumbles.

"You are a bunch of twisty-tailed coneheads!" their detailer hollered. "What type of greeting is that?"

"Good evening, Miss Shev...Cheev...Shayvray!" the mouse voices shouted.

Miss Chèvre singled out Bodie and had him repeat after her five times, her voice growing louder and his pronunciation worse with each try.

"I'm not doing it on purpose. There's no way to say that name!" Bodie sputtered in desperation to his squad mates when they were scurried off to a brief on officer development.

Only Ella, Victor, and Dilly had been able to pronounce Chèvre to her satisfaction, trilling the last syllable with a French accent. Ella's rodents were English harvest mice. Her horde had immigrated to the United States with another batch of mice from France, so it was no surprise she could pronounce the difficult name. Her accent was American Mouse, but every so often Chester could hear an inflection of her homeland in her voice. Victor was from Europe and had sampled a good bit of the creamy cheese, which made pronouncing her name a snap. Dilly admitted that it was his classical training in music that enabled him to enunciate the last tricky syllable.

"My grandfather sat me at his tail and taught me to sing using proper inflection," Dilly explained to his nestmates, who raised their brow whiskers at his ability. "Granddad played a stringed instrument, and we would sing together, along with my pop, all kinds of music, even some Italian opera!"

"This I gotta hear," Ranger had commented in wonder.

Dilly, though, was getting tired of being teased for his skill and razzed for bilging his shipmates. It was a matter of honor never to bilge or try to make yourself look better by showing off in front of your shipmates. Embarrassed at being singled out, Dilly attempted to teach Chester to say Chèvre.

"Try saying the second syllable with your tongue folded," Dilly suggested.

"Shev...Shevrala...yerlack...glack!" Chester tried several times.

"Okay, let's do this again. Say the first part of her name more like *Shay*, then clear your throat."

"Shay-verlack...*burr-gle*...glack..."

"Burgle? What are you doing?"

"I think I'm swallowing air."

"Start again, but his time put the back of your tongue on the roof of your mouth and pretend you've got a bit of popcorn imbedded there, and..."

"No."

"What?"

"*No*," Chester and Ranger said together.

"You're right, this is not working." Dilly gave up.

Ranger announced that he was not even going to try to say her name anymore, and he just got away with it by a whisker. One night they had hit the bulkhead, at attention, upright on their hind legs, being quizzed on their rates. Miss Chèvre stopped in front of Ranger and peppered him with professional knowledge questions.

"Yes, Miss Cheever!" he said in reply instead of "Ma'am, yes, ma'am!"

"What?" She glared into his face.

He had looked down from his superior height, his chunky front teeth exposed almost in a smile, and said under his breath into her surprised globe eyes, "How do you know I'm not saying it correctly?"

She had looked at him with open-mouthed astonishment, her whiskers twitching, and then moved on. Ranger's squad mates could never figure out how he got away with so many things.

They were all having a hard time with this unexpected obstacle to their training, and it frustrated Chester because their lives were hard enough.

Brown Bob was now released from SIQ. Following an examination by a medical mouse from the health department, he was allowed to attend and observe all company training, but he was not allowed to participate in anything more strenuous than marching, formation exercises, or squatting in the brief hall. He still had a bandage tied around his snout to protect the healing fracture. It drove him crazy to stand on the sidelines of the obstacle course when all the other plebe mice were grunting and running, pulling themselves over logs and scampering across wires and other obstacles set in their way. As Chester scraped along on his belly under thick vines poking out of the ground and pulled himself up to hurl his body over a gnarled branch, he caught a glimpse of Brown Bob standing idly by the side of the course. He could tell by the tension in his stance and the grim expression on his snout that the inactivity was eating at him, and Chester felt a little bad. On the other paw, he thought, *We are being trained in combat, and we all should expect injuries sometimes.* The truth was, Brown Bob was skilled in so many areas that he raged with frustration when he could not prove himself.

The new detailers had been with them for ten nights when they announced to the weary mice of Sixth Company that some of the plebe mice would be given the opportunity to show their leadership skills by commanding small recon teams to the Rooms Above and Below. Not every mouse would go. Only a small pawful would be chosen. All the plebe mice were anxious to have an opportunity to prove their ability. This was just the second time any of the plebes would be sent through the walls into the human living areas. There was excitement and heightened nerves as they all wondered who would go.

Ranger was exempted from the challenge because he was practicing daily for the fisticuff championship. Dilly was also excused because the mouse glee club was practicing their singing for a concert. Chester was gratified and gave a private little fist pump of victory when he was ordered not to report to the sailing center for his normal weeknight practice but to meet in the Ward Room at oh-dark-thirty. Only the upperclassmice were allowed to use the Ward Room for recreation, relaxation, and meetings, so it was exciting to be allowed into this inner sanctum.

Chester strode into the alcove, toes out, with a measured but quick pace, along with JP, Victor, Fleet, Bodie, Brown Bob, and some other rodents from Third, Fourth, and Fifth Companies. He looked around swiftly and wondered why these mice in particular had been selected from their companies.

Miss Chèvre stood with Mr. Cliff at the front of the gathering space, while other detailers milled around chatting. The plebes waited silently for their instructions, keeping their bearing, perched at ease, paws loosely curled at their sides, chins tucked, and faces wiped clean of any expression. They were never to show anger or fear or smile because it would bring a detailer down on them like a flyswatter.

At last Mr. Cliff called attention and revealed the objective. Mission leaders would be chosen from the group assembled. Each student leader would then be assigned two plebe mice from their own squads. A detailer would accompany them on their missions, but the student leaders would formulate the plans and give instructions to their teams.

They looked around the room out of the corner of their round eyes. Who would get to lead?

Mr. Cliff addressed Sixth Company first and called up Fleet to be a mission leader. Fleet looked smug as Bodie and JP were named to his team. Next Miss Chèvre chose Brown Bob to lead, with Chester and Victor as his team members.

Chester knew a lot of thought had gone into these selections. How much of his difficulties with Brown Bob had been noticed?

This challenge was designed to test their ability to lead and follow. If a mouse couldn't take orders, a mouse couldn't give orders. Chester was determined to be a strong link in the chain.

They clustered in teams and began planning. The mission had to be short because the night was almost over.

"Where do you plan to lead your team, Mr. Brown Bob?" Miss Chèvre asked.

"Ma'am, to human room number one three two four, ma'am," Brown Bob replied with confidence.

Chester remembered that room 1324 was the dormitory room Brown Bob had secretly snuck into during the first week of Plebe Summer to get a replacement drill pretzel for Bodie.

"What is your objective? What do you wish to obtain?" she continued.

"Ma'am, we are going to get supplies for the Sixth Company Ward Room, ma'am."

Brown Bob must have figured this would please the detailers because they held all their meetings there. They would enjoy some extra tasty snacks. After approving his plan, Miss Chèvre informed Brown Bob that due to his injury, he would not be able to do any of the physical work of rooting around in closets or high climbing during the mission.

*That has got to rub Brown Bob's fur the wrong way,* Chester thought. Maybe Brown Bob had been selected as team leader because of his injury. Chester knew Brown Bob too would suspect that. Now Brown Bob would really want to prove himself.

Miss Chèvre instructed him to give each team member their orders, including herself. Brown Bob would certainly have to think on his feet.

"Chester, you will search the locker next to the desk on one side of the room, and Victor, you will search on the other side of the room. I will point to these places once we have penetrated into the interior."

He paused, waited, and then Miss Chèvre gave a little ahem. He looked at her.

"You—"

"Who? Address me properly!" she said, whiskers twitching.

Brown Bob stood stock still. The seconds ticked. Swiftly he turned to Victor. "Victor, you will relay all orders from me to Miss...to Miss...Tell her she is to stand ready to receive supplies and secure them outside the room."

Victor turned smartly to their detailer. "Miss Chèvre," he said, saying her name easily, flourishing the last syllable, which sounded as if he had a little something stuck in the back of his throat.

*Brilliant,* Chester thought with admiration. *That was quick thinking.*

"Miss Chèvre, you will stand ready to receive supplies and secure them outside the room."

Brown Bob led them back to their wing and down the pipes and wiring he had discovered weeks before. They entered room 1324 through a small hole in the back of one of the closets. Chester smelled the humans and a strong cheese aroma. *Jackpot.* Brown Bob's target was right on.

They moved out of the closet across the center of the room to the furthest wall. Brown Bob gestured for Victor to climb up the closet doors and search the open cabinets. He respectfully motioned for Miss Chèvre to stand watch below. He then took Chester back to the cabinets and lockers closest to their escape hole and pointed for him to begin searching the unlocked interiors.

Chester shimmied up the closet edge and wedged himself into the darkness. He sniffed and explored in the cupboard, but every-thing seemed to be enclosed in very hard, impenetrable material.

He came out and motioned to Brown Bob waiting below that there was nothing there, by holding his front paws up with a shrug of the shoulders. Brown Bob frowned and pointed a claw to the desk. Chester dropped to the floor, scurried across on all fours, climbed up a chair leg, and leaped from seat to chair arm to desktop. Again, nothing. Everything was pristine and clean. Across the room Chester could see Victor and Miss Chèvre gesturing to each other from the floor where she was standing to the bookcase above the desk where Victor was perched. He held a large cherry cough drop in his paws, ready to toss it down.

On the floor Brown Bob was sniffing furiously, following the pungent odor of cheese. He scouted to the other side of the chair by the desk where Chester sat on his haunches awaiting orders, following the aroma of extra-sharp cheddar. He motioned firmly for Chester to investigate the origin of the smell, pantomiming an exaggerated sniffing and walking movement. Chester saw a narrow gangplank leading from the chair over a deep abyss and felt a sense of unease. A huge chunk of cheese seemed to balance in the air at the end of what looked like a flat piece of wood. He motioned to Brown Bob that he wasn't sure he liked the layout.

*I smell a rat,* he thought.

Brown Bob strongly motioned him to continue, backing up to get a better view of where Chester was pointing. Chester hopped down to the chair and had just begun sidling out onto the ruler when Miss Chèvre turned around with her cough drop and spied the crude trap that had been hidden from her view.

"Nooo!" she shrieked just as Chester tipped the balance of the wooden ruler and plunged headlong into the bottom of the can with a thunk.

Victor saw the whole thing happen from where he stood on the shelf. Miss Chèvre dropped her cough drop and ran to the garbage can. Brown Bob had already pulled himself up to the top of the chair and was peering down into the darkness.

"Chester…Chester!" he called.

"I'm down here," Chester's voice echoed back.

"Are you hurt?" Brown Bob's voice was tense.

"I don't think so."

"Can you get out?" Brown Bob called again.

"The walls are slippery. I can't get a claw hold."

"Try jumping!"

Chester kept jumping, sliding back down the sides after each attempt. His breath was coming in quick puffs; he was fighting down the panic. He had to get out of there.

Miss Chèvre's voice repeated, "This is bad…this is bad…"

"Try propping up the ruler. Climb up, then jump. Victor! Find a rope!" Chester heard Brown Bob whispering sharp orders.

There was loud rustling and a thud in the room. A light flicked on, and he heard a human shout. Chester squinted in the bright glare. Brown Bob had disappeared from the chair edge. A shadow fell across the bottom of the can, and Chester looked up. There in the wide opening was a huge human face with brown eyes and very short brown hair peering down at him. This was one of their compatriots from the Rooms Below, a fellow naval officer in training. Chester sat up on his haunches and peered back intently, black eyes blinking in the light, whiskers twitching. He gave the biggest grin he could muster to show he was friendly since he wasn't in uniform.

A large hand reached into the can, causing Chester to shrink back against the side. He heard great rumblings of voices. The ruler was removed, and then the lights went out.

❧

B. Wise leaped down from his rack. Now he had to decide what to do with the rodent in his trash can. T. Briggs climbed down from his rack in two quick steps, and they both leaned over Wise's trap. All up and down the hallway, they could hear the harsh voices of the detailers yelling, stirring everyone out of their beds. It was just past dawn.

"Did you see how many mice there were when I turned on the light last night?" B. Wise asked his roommate.

"I was zonked. But I did see one run under your closet door. What are you going to do with the one you caught?"

"I don't know. I decided to wait until morning to figure out how to get rid of it. There was no way it could escape."

B. Wise looked at the small tawny-colored mouse huddled in the bottom of the can.

"He looks harmless, but you should have seen the way it bared its teeth at me when I reached in to take the ruler out of the trap!"

"So what do we do now?" Briggs asked. He scratched his back rapidly as he yawned and reached for his blue-rimmed T-shirt.

B. Wise was still staring down into the can when one of the new yellow-shirted detailers barged into their room.

"What are you guys doing? You should be dressed and shaved!" The detailer glanced into B. Wise's wastebasket. "Hey, you guys caught a mouse. Where's it going: Jump School or Dive School?"

Wise and Briggs looked at him with a blank stare.

"Flush or skydive?" the upperclassman asked again.

Neither of the roommates replied. The detailer glanced around the room. Catching sight of B. Wise's toy parachute soldiers sitting neatly on top of his desk, he took action. "It's Jump School then."

The first-class midshipman with the yellow shirt reached into the can, grabbed the creature by the scruff of its neck, and ordered T. Briggs to assist.

"Open the window!"

He made little ceremony of flinging the tiny mouse from the upper floor into the morning air.

"You've got thirty seconds to be ready and dressed!" he barked at the two incredulous plebes before he strode out of the room.

"Well, that was a little harsh," B. Wise said reproachfully.

CHAPTER 16

# An Apparition

❧

SIXTH COMPANY WAS IN AN uproar. Although the plebe mice were confined to their nests, they still milled about their quarters, claws scratching and tails thumping the floorboards, even though it was well past time for them to be asleep. Yellow-shirted detailers, fur fluffing around the collars, scurried up and down the p-way, their long tails whipping behind them as they were called to emergency briefings.

Ranger and Dilly perched upright, balancing by a paw on the beams of their nest entrance, peering down the passage, wondering where Chester was. They had heard a rumor but could not believe it was true. Brown Bob and Victor had returned from the training mission, but Chester had not. Some mouse whispered that Brown Bob, Victor, and Miss Chèvre were closeted with the superintendent of midshipmice and were being questioned. For what?

After an anxious few minutes, they saw Victor come slowly down the passage, walking alone. As he passed their nest, Ranger and Dilly gestured urgently to him and then dragged Victor in before they could be told to disperse and get in their racks.

"Where is he? What's happened to Chester?"

Victor shook his head sadly, pink ears flattened to his deep-gray cone-shaped head. His round eyes behind the black glasses seemed even larger than usual. He spread his forepaws out and gave a little shrug.

"We don't know. The last I saw him, he had plunged into the bottom of a devilish marauder trap."

"*What?*" Dilly uttered in dismay.

"So"—Ranger was in a fury—"why didn't you get him out?"

"We were trying. I was just beginning to chew off the rope when two large feet stomped across the floor near where I was working, and the lights came on. Miss Chèvre screamed for us to evacuate. Brown Bob was nearly swatted off the chair. We were being chased! I think our friends below mistook us for marauders!"

"Don't tell me you left!" Dilly was in shock.

"Brown Bob and I tried to convince Miss Chèvre to allow us time to think. We were arguing hotly outside the escape hole, but she insisted we return. She was reciting protocol, nearly hysterical."

"And you listened to her?" Dilly was getting wild.

"I was taking orders, Dilly." For once the foreign mouse sounded almost American.

"What did the supe say?" Ranger asked Victor, referring to the superintendent of midshipmice.

"He was trying to find out how the incident had occurred. He was quite rough on Miss Chèvre. She will probably be brought before a review board. Brown Bob was grinding his teeth. He kept repeating that it was his fault and that he took full responsibility."

Dilly plopped his slim fawn-colored body down to all fours and looked at Chester's empty rack. He felt a lump starting in his throat.

"We gotta do something, Ranger," he said.

Ranger was rummaging through his cubby, pulling out boxing gear, extra piles of issued clothes, his sailor-cup cap, blue camo shirts, and other issued items.

"Aha," he finally said, "here it is." In his paw he held a long, coiled piece of rope.

"Where did you get that?" Dilly asked.

"It was an extra length lying around after the rope-climb exercise. Thought it might come in handy. Did a bit of mountain rappelling when I was an enlisted mouse. Never know when I'll want to take it up again." Ranger wound the twine around his short front leg and up and over his shoulder as he spoke.

"Count me in. Let's get him out of there," Dilly said as he stood up and faced his roommate, short blond whiskers held still by his clenched jaw.

"I will go too. What do you have in mind?" Victor asked.

"I think we will improvise when we get there. Victor, you are going to have to show us where it happened. With luck Chester will still be, will still be...will still be where we can get to him."

The trio were moving purposefully toward the entrance just as Mr. Cliff stepped into the doorway accompanied by a chaplain. Mr. Cliff surveyed the three and the rope coiled on Ranger's shoulder and drew the right conclusion.

"Sorry, rodents. Can't allow it. Everyone is to stay in quarters."

He actually sounded understanding instead of threatening.

Dilly spoke out of turn, respectful but firm. "Sir, excuse me, sir...our nestmate is missing. We must attempt a rescue. We know where he is."

Mr. Cliff sighed. His round light-brown ears were thick and tough, but they flattened for a moment before they perked once again. He faced the agitated plebe mice with his white underbelly pulled upright.

"Follow orders," he said firmly.

"We've got to try! You can't mean you are just going to leave him there!" Dilly was now pacing.

The chaplain motioned for the three mice to sit down while Mr. Cliff shared what information he could.

"There is a rescue team being assembled right now. Let those with more training go in. This is a delicate mission. We cannot threaten the balance, which we have maintained with the humans for more than a hundred years, by barging into their daytime territory. They are awake now."

The chaplain put out a calming paw. "Let me sit and wait with you."

Just then Ella slipped quietly into the room. She paused when she saw the detailer and a strange adult mouse. The chaplain motioned for her to come in. Mr. Cliff told her to sit as she had immediately snapped to swift attention.

"Any news?" she whispered. "It can't be true!"

"It's true," Ranger and Dilly said at the same time.

It was hard to tell when a mouse face blanched, but Ella definitely lost color. Her triangular head shrunk down into the ribbon of white fur around her neck.

"Oh no," she moaned softly.

At that moment a rustle was heard in the entranceway. Bursting through the wooden posts that held the nesting material neatly aside, came an apparition, bearing bundles of mysterious objects and covered in debris.

It was Chester.

"Guess what!" he shouted jubilantly to the assembled mice. "I went to Jump School!"

The five mice crammed into the small nest gasped aloud. Next to her Ella heard the chaplain whisper, "Thank you! We've never lost one yet. At least not during Plebe Summer."

Had she looked, she would have seen the chaplain turn his eyes heavenward. But everyone was dumbstruck at the appearance of

Chester, dirt and twigs snagged in his fur, bits of string wrapped snuggly about his body, and holding a crumpled wad of clear, crinkly cellophane. Even more mysterious was a large dark-green plastic human statue clutched in his paw, which he dragged behind him.

Dilly sprang forward and flattened Chester to the ground with a leaping hug. Ranger jumped on top as they hugged and squeaked.

They were so well trained that they shot to their hind legs when Mr. Cliff called smartly, "Attention on deck! What happened, plebe mouse?"

Chester pulled himself together and told his story. He shared how he had fallen into the trap set for marauders when he had attempted to retrieve the cheese lying at the end of a ruler. He had not been hurt, only bruised, when he plummeted to the bottom of the wastebasket. He had heard his friends calling and then saw Brown Bob appear at the chair seat edge.

"He was shouting for me to climb up the ruler and jump. I tried to jump to the lip of the can but was unable to leap far enough." He paused in the story to look at Ella. "I bet you could have done it."

She smiled slightly and shrugged her shoulders modestly.

"Then the lights went on in the room, and my team disappeared. A *huge* human face appeared over the top of the opening."

Chester explained that even though he was terrified at the misunderstanding, he had smiled broadly at this fellow future naval officer to show he was friendly.

"Then the human removed the ruler and turned out the light, and I was alone."

Chester stopped and stared without focus as he remembered the next part of the story. He didn't share the shock he felt in the moments after his recon team left and the humans went back to their beds, leaving him in the trash bin. They were the most difficult minutes of his life. He hadn't even been tempted to eat the cheese left sitting next to him. He had wondered what would happen to him. He thought about Mama and Papa, Grandfather, Allie-Poo, Bean, Theo, Dilly, and Ranger.

He was silent as he worked through that part of the adventure. Dilly and Ranger waited, quiet, imagining how frightening it must have been.

"Then what happened?" Mr. Cliff prompted him.

Chester continued with his story.

"The sun began to rise. The two humans leaped out of their beds to the sound of bangs and shouts just as fast as we are awakened every night." Chester nodded respectfully at Mr. Cliff. "Two big faces peered into my prison. I tried to communicate my situation, but they didn't seem to understand. The next thing I knew, another large human appeared, wearing a yellow shirt just like our detailers." Chester acknowledged Mr. Cliff with another nod.

"He picked me up by the scruff of my neck"—*which I hated*, he thought—"and I was whirled around in the air getting dizzy until he got me situated."

"Situated?"

Chester explained that while he was hanging in the air, he saw the huge yellow-shirted arm reach out and grab an object off the desk where he had been scouting earlier that night. He remembered seeing a little pile of plastic human statues attached to clear umbrella-shaped pouches with thin white strings.

"Parachute men. They're toys." Mr. Cliff nodded wisely.

Chester nodded back and continued his tale.

"The immense human detailer wrapped the string from the parachute snug around my middle. The next thing I knew I was sailing out the window! The wind caught the chute and sent me sideways for quite a distance. I had to direct my descent by pulling

and tugging the strings this way and that. The sun was so bright I had to squint, and I just barely missed being snagged in the green leaves of a treetop. I managed to dodge it at the last second."

"Sounds like fun!" the fluffy-cheeked chaplain was inspired to say.

Chester smiled to himself when he remembered how he had been blown straight past a squirrel sitting on a branch and had given the startled creature a smart salute.

"Go on," Mr. Cliff urged.

"It was a bit of a rough landing; I hit the ground, then was dragged, skidding and bumping, collecting bits of sticks and dirt along the way. I think I lost a patch of fur!" he mentioned proudly.

Ranger and Dilly peered with interest at his backside, which Chester rubbed with a paw.

"Continue," Mr. Cliff prompted, starting to sound a little impatient.

"I was unfamiliar with the area where I landed. Everything looks different in the daylight. I was still by Bancroft Hall but couldn't find an entrance. I had to gnaw off the chute and green statue, then search for a hole. Once I found one, it took a while to get my bearings. I ran into a mouse on watch who sent me in the right direction, and here I am!"

Mr. Cliff stood, every whisker of his snout taut with purpose. "I have to alert the commandant to call off the search. Well done, plebe mouse."

Mr. Cliff left so fast he forgot to tell Ella to return to her nest. The chaplain rose and spoke a few words of gratitude and relief, promising he would be available if any of them needed to speak with him further. When he left, the friends were finally alone.

Dilly and Ranger oohed and aahed over the green human statue and propped him in a corner of their nest. Ranger studied the cellophane parachute intently. He arched a brow whisker at Chester, and Chester winked back. Ranger quickly rolled and folded the chute and stowed it in a secret cranny in their nest.

"This could come in handy someday." He grinned.

"Why do you think the humans sent you out the window like that?" Ella asked. It was the question everyone had to be thinking.

"I heard their detailer say I was to be sent to Dive School or Jump School," Chester answered. "So obviously they did recognize me as a fellow midshipmouse! I think they were trying to help me evade enemies or expedite my return," Chester continued. "And I think I know a way to repay their kindness."

⚜

B. Wise dashed into his room and stowed his rifle in the locker, making sure to clasp the dangling chain.

He glanced at the window and even went over to crane his neck to see if he could see down to the ground. Briggs came running in behind him, tearing off his cover, rifle, and other gear.

"What're you looking at?"

"Nothing. I wonder what happened to that little fella. Can't see him down there."

"Of course not. It's gone. We've seen the last of that pest."

CHAPTER 17

# Losing a Plebe Mouse

❖

CHESTER WAS A HERO. EVERYONE stopped him to ask his story or scurried into the nest to peer at the large green military man. Ranger and Dilly told the story of his appearing in the doorway over and over, but mostly everyone wanted to know what it was like to fall into the trap, to be so close to the humans, and especially to have experienced a parachute jump. Chester was the first to go to Jump School.

Chester didn't like talking about the lonely hours in the wastebasket, but he was gracious about the two midshipmen whose room he had shared in the wee hours before dawn.

The next night Mr. Cliff appeared after Chester had awakened from sleep to inform him that Captain Thunder, the commandant of midshipmice, desired to meet with him for a debriefing.

"Captain Thunder wishes to speak to you himself. No chain of command on this one. The dant is a very busy mouse. When he has a clear moment in his schedule, you will receive a summons. The uniform will be white alphas. You will proceed immediately and not keep him waiting. You will approach his space and address him in the proper way."

Chester gulped. "Sir, yes, sir."

This sounded serious. Would he be reprimanded for nearly having to be rescued again? Would the dant tell him he had made too many mistakes and ask him to leave? When would he receive the summons?

Everything was happening so quickly; there was no time to recover from the adventure. Detailers screamed at them every night on the drill field. Plebe Summer was almost over, and soon they would be marching in their first formal parade in front of their families and invited special dignitaries. At some point they would be deemed fit to meet the rest of the Brigade of Midshipmice.

A few nights later, Chester's squad was assigned to damage control. The mice gathered in a basement area wearing their foul-weather gear. They were taught how to staunch the flow of water from leaky pipes as if they were in a flooding ship or submarine. Detailer mice then taught them to lift a sink nozzle in teams and aim the jet of water at an imaginary fire. It was messy, wet, exhausting work. The odor of mouse fur was pungent.

Chester had been looking for Brown Bob ever since their recon mission, but he had not been at any of their meals or drills since the incident. Perhaps his snout had been injured again during the panic after he fell into the trap. He wanted to let him know he was fine and to thank him for standing by and attempting to get him out of the trash can.

It wasn't until two nights later that he heard the news. Brown Bob was going Tango.

Every mouse was in shock. Bodie had been mysteriously quiet, but he finally opened up. Brown Bob had come back from his interview with the supe the night of Chester's disappearance, grinding and squeaking his teeth. Throwing himself into his rack, all he would tell Bodie was that it was all his fault; he never should have told Chester to go after the cheese.

No one could believe this was happening. Brown Bob was one of the strongest, most well-liked, and confident of the plebe mice.

Rumor spread that he had told the superintendent he felt it was best to leave and had asked to be separated. Brown Bob was being counseled and given time to think it through, but for now he was assigned to Tango Company. For some reason he was not removed from the nest he shared with Bodie and sent to different quarters. He was absent for training at night and slept there during the day.

Chester was stunned.

Ranger, who had just come back from winning his second preliminary fisticuff match, shook his head. "Waste of a good mouse."

Dilly whistled through his teeth and looked troubled. Chester kept thinking.

At dawn, when the mice had sung "Blue and Gold," finished their last duty for the night, and dropped into their nests, Chester made a decision. He crept out of his rack as the sky outside turned pearly gray and skittered noiselessly down to Bodie and Brown Bob's nest. Bodie was curled up in a great mound, already snoring. There was no movement from the other rack. As he moved closer, he saw Brown Bob's glistening eyes and pointy face staring at the ceiling. He could hear the slight squeak of his grinding teeth.

"Yo, B," Chester said casually.

"Hey."

There was silence, and then Brown Bob uttered one word: "Sorry."

"For what?"

"Almost getting you killed."

Brown Bob turned on his side, facing the twigs and string of the nest wall.

"You did what you had to do; you were leading a mission for food."

Brown Bob turned back suddenly. "No, I was saving face. I wanted to be the hero. I wanted to show I was a leader."

Chester remembered his own hour of darkness in the chapel and squatted down on the floor.

"Did you *know* the cheese was a trap?"

"No, but—"

"Would you make the same mistake again if you saw the same trap?"

"Of course not…"

"Well, what makes you different from any other rodent here?"

Brown Bob sat up.

"I thought I *was* different…but let's see…I nearly lost the small boat challenge—"

"My fault," Chester graciously conceded, "and we weren't the only ones."

"I lost in the first round of the bare-knuckle Fisticuff Competition *and* broke my snout!"

Chester shrugged slightly.

"And in trying to make up for it, I put you in a bucket and everyone else in danger. A fine officer I would make. My brothers would never have done that."

Brown Bob was no longer the glamorous, tough rodent he had always seemed to Chester. He was just like all the others.

"Have you asked your brothers about their failures?" Chester asked quietly.

"Oh, I don't have to. Gray Bob and Beau Bob are top-notch officers. They never failed."

"You didn't either, Brown Bob. You tried to rescue me."

"It's not enough."

There was silence as Bodie snored and Brown Bob pulled his paws close to his chest in tight fists.

"You're a strong link in the chain. None of us wants you to leave," Chester finally offered.

Brown Bob snorted painfully through his swollen snout. "It sure hasn't gone the way I thought it would."

⚜

B. Wise and T. Briggs stood in front of the only mirror in their quarters wearing their new dress white uniforms and trying to figure out how to attach the straps that would keep their shirts neatly tucked into the pants. The elastic bands were connected by a clip from their shirttails and ran down their legs to attach at the top of their socks.

"This is weird," Briggs commented.

"Think it's going to rub the hair off my legs!" Wise whistled at his roommate. "Lookin' good, Briggsy!"

They admired themselves in the mirror and then prepared to leave the room for inspection. B. Wise gave a last look at the silver *E* and bronze *S* pinned into the ribbon bar above his breast pocket.

"Missed that *E* in rifle by only a few shots," he muttered in aggravation at himself, but he was very proud of his expert rating in pistol firing.

He glanced at the white sailor blouse thrown over his desk chair, looking forward to the end of the week when he would never have to wear it again. T. Briggs peered into their trash can.

"No more traps, Wise?"

"No. It nearly made me sick, seeing that little fellow flung out the window! I'll keep everything tightly sealed in plastic bins from now on."

B. Wise fiddled with the bicycle lock that still dangled from his rifle locker.

"Sure wish I could get a regulation lock before alpha room inspection."

"Doubt there's time."

"It's humiliating. And I wanted my parents to see my side of the room in perfect order." Wise looked at his desk; all his books lined up largest to smallest, surface shiny and clean. "When are your parents arriving, Briggs?"

"Probably Thursday night. They said they'd be here for the whole weekend. The parade on Friday for sure. They're really excited for the opportunity to tour Bancroft Hall."

"Mine too. They want to see if I keep my room neater here than at home!" B. Wise looked again at his dangling bicycle lock and grimaced. "Oh well, they'll be allowed in again in two years...I should have a new lock by then," he said with sarcasm. "Hey, man, can you believe Plebe Summer is almost over?"

"Not soon enough! I'll be glad to have contact with the outside world again and get rid of our detailers."

"Yeah, but the rest of the brigade will be coming back in a week, and Mother B. will be crawling with upperclassmen, so no break there."

T. Briggs sighed. "Out of the frying pan and into the fire!"

"What?" Wise laughed at his roommate's choice of words.

"I mean we will be getting out of a bad situation and into a worse one."

"Come on, Briggsy, don't be so pessimistic!"

CHAPTER 18

# Out of The Whirlwind

⚜

CHESTER SKITTERED AS FAST AS he was allowed, without actually running, to meet Captain Thunder, the commandant of midshipmice, in his office. The plebe mice all admired the dant. He was known to be fair, encouraging, and a great leader. Still Chester was nervous and could feel the sweat forming under his whiskers and behind his round ears. No one had reprimanded him or hinted at a bad report, but he still wondered if he could be sent home.

He had left Dilly with Ranger, who had just changed his clothes for the Fisticuff Smoker and was practice kicking with his powerful haunches and doing stretches on the floor of their nest. Chester had clapped Ranger on the back and told him they all believed he would bring home the medal for Sixth Company. He also told him he wasn't sure if would return in time for the match.

Now Chester stood outside the first-floor space, near the rotunda, listening for the chime of the clock tower on the Yard, marking the time of his appointment. At the final tone of the bells, he gave a loud ahem, knocked, received the go-ahead from the commandant's assistant, and strode through the hole in the wall. The uniformed assistant led him to another hole and gestured for him to pass through. Chester took a deep breath, entered into the dant's office, and announced himself.

"Sir! This is Midshipmouse Fourth-Class Chester. Permission to come aboard, sir!"

Captain Thunder rose with a smile while Chester stood at attention.

"Permission granted. At ease! Have a seat."

Chester maintained his bearing by not smiling in return.

"Yes, sir!" he replied firmly and sat down on the edge of a stool. Even seated, his furry body was upright and stiff, tail curved at the proper angle.

Captain Thunder didn't waste a minute with pleasantries. "I've been given the details of your interaction with the humans a few nights ago. You acted courageously and appropriately in the situation. You remained dedicated to the mission; you adapted and improvised even in the midst of potential danger to yourself."

Chester's head was spinning. "Sir, yes, sir" was all he could think to say.

"Your quick return to your quarters saved the rescue team from being exposed. So how was your first parachute jump?"

Chester was surprised by the question. He had expected to be quizzed as to how he ended up in the bottom of a trash can and reprimanded for finding himself there. The plebe mice often said that even if a problem wasn't strictly your fault, you were to blame if you were found within a mile of the incident. Chester brought his mind back to the parachute jump.

"I didn't really have time to think about it in the moment, sir, but it was an experience I wish to repeat one day."

"Perhaps you'll have that opportunity...I understand that the soldier statue remains in your quarters. I've authorized your detailers to allow you to keep it. Maybe you could donate it to the Naval Mouse Museum once you graduate from the academy?"

"Sir, yes, sir. Thank you, sir!" Chester was almost dizzy from relief.

"I also understand the parachute has disappeared."

Now Chester began to sweat uncomfortably. He was just about to admit its whereabouts when Captain Thunder lowered his voice.

"Keep it," he whispered with a wink. "Your name has been put in for a commendation, Mr. Chester," Captain Thunder continued. "Is there anything you'd like to tell me about the experience?"

"Yes, sir, there is." Chester began to relax a little. "I learned something while I was in the human room below, and I think the humans treated me kindly—I would like to return that kindness."

"Tell me about it."

"The weights we use for our combat course are devices they use to lock up their rifle closets. One of the humans is missing his lock on his cupboard. The other human has one. I saw this as I rummaged through their storage cabinets. One has a lock with a loose chain that doesn't quite close the door properly. The humans treated me with honor by sending me swiftly back to safety. I'd like to repay them by returning one of the weights to their room."

Captain Thunder rubbed his furry angled jaw and considered Chester appraisingly. Chester sat uncomfortably as the seconds ticked by.

"Good observation, plebe." He continued to ponder Chester's request and then nodded his head with decision.

"You know, I think you've got something here. We do not want any strain on the relationship we have maintained with the humans for more than one hundred years. This could be a way to heal the breach that occurred the other night. I have also been wondering how the experience might have affected you mentally by the near…by the time you spent alone in the trap. We discussed getting you back down into the rooms quickly to lessen any negative impact. Here is what we are going to do—I am putting you in charge of a mission to return a lock. Mr. Cliff will go with you, but you may choose three other plebe mice to be on your team."

"Sir, yes, sir! Thank you, sir!" Chester's heart was racing with excitement. "I already have three in mind: Ranger, Dilly, and Brown Bob."

Captain Thunder had been nodding, but at the last name, his whiskers fell. "That's a bad business about Brown Bob. He can't take part in any activities while he's Tango. We're hoping he'll reconsider, but he's still asking for separation."

"He doesn't belong in Tango Company," Chester voiced calmly and with authority. "He just doesn't know it's okay to fail."

"I'll talk with his commanding officer, but I'd come up with another name if I were you. In any case I want this lock business taken care of tonight."

"Sir, tell him we don't go unless he goes, sir."

The older mouse smiled at Chester's resolute insistence. "I think you have the makings of a fine officer, Chester."

Captain Thunder rose and dismissed Chester, telling him to get to Dahlgren Hall quickly. They would both be in time to watch the majority of the Fisticuff Competition.

The yellow flags were flying high in front of the thirty companies of mice squatted upon the gymnasium floor. The midshipmice were shouting and cheering wildly. Their collective competitive spirit and the anticipation of the end of Plebe Summer in just a few short nights was bringing the room to a fevered pitch.

Chester found a spot in between JP and Fleet and shimmied in.

"What's happening?" he asked.

"Ranger's still in. He's had three fights. How'd it go with the dant?" JP asked.

Word had spread about his meeting. Just as Chester was going to say how well it had gone, a roar sounded in the gymnasium. The fisticuff champs from Twenty-Eighth and Thirteenth Companies were both knocked out of the competition in two separate rings. Fleet leaned over and spoke into Chester's round ear. He could feel the hot breath on his neck.

"Did the dant say it's your fault that Brown Bob is leaving? Some rodents are saying that."

Chester turned his snout and looked with surprise at Fleet, taken aback by the sharp words.

"No!" he replied, curt and stunned.

"Don't listen to him. He's an idiot."

Chester turned his head to look at JP, equally surprised by his aggressive tone. JP was usually a peacemaker, a quiet leader. Now JP was on the offense, defending Chester against his nestmate. Chester realized how much he had learned about his shipmates over Plebe Summer and how much they had all been changed by the experience. Still there was one thing he did not know about JP.

He shouted above the crowd, "JP, what do your initials stand for?"

"John Paul," JP shouted back. "I was named after my great-great-grandfather. We were both named after a human naval hero—John Paul Jones. My ancestors saw his name inscribed in the chapel."

Chester was impressed by his fine lineage, but mostly he was impressed by JP's quiet confidence.

Chester and JP quickly turned their attention back to the fights, where they saw Ranger moving about the ring. He was fighting with a large gray mouse from Twentieth Company. The mice of Sixth Company leaped to their feet, chattering and chanting encouragement. Dilly, who was their standard bearer, was waving the yellow flag. The skirmish was over in a minute; Ranger had won again.

Chester looked to the raised area where the officers were sitting. Captain Thunder was not among the group. The dant was normally at all the plebe mouse functions. He had just dismissed Chester from his office with the encouragement that they both should hurry over. Why wasn't he there?

The fighters were down to four—Ranger and the company champs from Third, Ninth, and Seventeenth Companies. They were paired up to decide who would fight in the final round.

Once again the noise was deafening as the entire roomful of mice leaped to their feet, tails slapping the floor, voices squeaking shrilly. Toward the front of Sixth Company, Chester spotted Dilly cheering wildly for Ranger, who was making good progress in his match. He looked around at the sea of familiar furry faces, feeling so much a part of this group of rodents. What if Fleet was right? Did they really blame him for Brown Bob's decision to leave?

He glanced again at the officers on the step. Captain Thunder appeared. He was saying hello to the supe, clapping a firm paw on his shoulder and nodding to the others around him. Just as Chester was about to look away, he saw Captain Thunder scan the room, bulging eyes stopping at the Sixth Company flag and roving back and forth until they locked onto Chester. There was a fair distance between them, but he knew Captain Thunder was looking for him. Flustered, he turned his pink nose back to the fight. Ranger made a swift move, blocked and punched. Just as he opened his snout to shout, he felt a paw on his shoulder and a muscular body pushed in between him and Fleet. He turned to make room and looked straight into Brown Bob's glossy, round eyes.

"Brown Bob!" he gasped.

"Yeah, rodent."

Everyone was yelling and cheering for Ranger, who had just won his match. Those immediately surrounding Chester were nudging and jostling Brown Bob with glad smiles and somewhat shy welcoming words. They didn't know what to make of his sudden appearance.

Chester looked back at the group of officers only to realize that Captain Thunder was still looking with purpose his way. When their eyes met, the dant gave a nod and, Chester could swear, a wink.

"I think you and I have a mission tonight," Brown Bob said loudly.

"Yeah, yes, we do," Chester responded with a smile curving up underneath his whiskers.

Brown Bob slapped his shoulder again, and they both turned toward the center ring, where the final fisticuff fight was about to take place between Ranger and a broad-chested, multicolored mouse from Seventeenth Company. The opponents were squaring off, both looking determined but a little weary. For once Ranger did not have his customary wide-angle grin.

Chester heard Fleet shout to Brown Bob, "Glad you're back! What happened? Forgive and forget, huh?"

Brown Bob's shiny head swiveled. All Chester could hear was a snarl.

"You don't know what the rat's nest you're talking about."

"No harm, no harm!" Fleet's voice was indrawn and conciliatory. He turned back to the match, his normal haughty expression wiped from his white snout.

The bout was fierce and wild. Ranger and his rival were locked and reeling across the marked-out area. Neither mouse was giving an inch to the other. Suddenly Ranger slipped out from under the other's grasping claw, dropped a shoulder, and feigned a punch with his left foot and then swung powerfully with his right haunch into a brutal body blow. It was all over in a second. The plebe mice erupted into a roar as Ranger's paw was held up by the officiating detailer and declared the winner.

"The move you taught him!" Chester shouted into Brown Bob's ear as they were swept forward by the members of Sixth Company pressing to get close to the front. Brown Bob gave him a brilliant grin, exposing his two large upper teeth.

"Yeah, that's mine!"

Chester pushed and wiggled to get up to the ring to congratulate Ranger, but in the back of his mind, he was thinking nonstop. In a few short hours, he would be leading his friends on a mission to return the lock. His head reeled with ideas of how to carry the heavy metal weight down to the human midshipman room below. He discarded one idea after the other. It would be tricky.

Just before dawn, Chester, Dilly, Ranger, and Brown Bob scurried with purposeful steps to meet Mr. Cliff at the prearranged spot. As they approached the duty desk, Chester saw a young plebe mouse and another uniformed rodent perched together behind the cube of yellow sticky notes, which served as their workspace and communication center. The skinny, silent plebe mouse finished writing a message on the top sheet, ripped it from the large yellow block with two paws, and handed it to the uniformed rodent. The brown rodent received it and turned. It was Spleen. Chester sucked in his breath.

Mr. Cliff called out in a confident, bantering tone. "What are you doing here, Spleen? Back from third block so soon? This is the Sixth Company hallway; Fifth Company is the other way."

"Cool your whiskers; wouldn't be here if I didn't have to be— Sixth Company doesn't compare with Fifth, and you know it." Spleen's reply was curt. "Got back from my summer training block, and I've been assigned to help coordinate reform. Going around to all the companies and getting their final numbers."

"Where were you?" Mr. Cliff remained polite.

"Mag-taf: mouse air and ground task force."

Spleen turned his drab snout and surveyed the group of plebe mice gathered around Mr. Cliff. His eyes stopped at Chester and narrowed. "What's this, your reject squad? I thought this rodent would be gone by now." He jerked his thick leathery ears toward Chester.

Chester stood still. Deep inside he felt a spark of anger that surprised him at its intensity. *I do not deserve this. I have earned my place here.* He felt the stiffening of his friends around him. All eyes were locked on Spleen, and no one flicked a whisker.

"These are some of my best," Cliff answered in his regular clipped manner.

"You've got to be kidding me." Spleen pointed a brown claw at Chester and said, "Not this one."

"Especially this one." Mr. Cliff stared down Spleen.

"Good luck with that," Spleen replied.

Mr. Cliff ushered them away from the desk. As soon as they were out of earshot, he spoke to Chester. "I don't know what you did to get on his bad side, but do your best to stay out of his way. Spleen will be a great warrior, every mouse thinks so, but he has a nasty temper. I'll give him this: he sets the bar high, and he lives up to it. He doesn't think any other mouse can, I guess. He's in Fifth Company, so he shouldn't be able to bother you during the academic year. C'mon, let's get this mission done."

Chester let his breath out in a long stream from the side of his snout. That was the most information he had ever heard Mr. Cliff utter. He remembered when he received his company number on INight. The kind old mouse in charge of the box of assignments had held out a square of paper with Fifth Company scratched out and Sixth Company written in. Had he remained in Fifth Company he would have been toast. Burnt toast.

Chester assembled his team around the jagged gap in the floor that overlooked the space in the wall outside the room below. Mr. Cliff stood by, watching all their movements. Ranger held the coil of rope from his secret stash over a shoulder, Dilly gripped a large piece of blanket, and Brown Bob had a long pencil clutched under his foreleg.

The four had dragged the heavy metal lock down their hallway on the blanket, allowing it to slide easily. Now they stood over the entrance hole, waiting to see how Chester intended to bring it to the floor below. Chester picked up a mysterious circular piece of plastic with a large hole in the center, which he had laid next to the entry spot earlier. He explained that it was the inside of a tape dispenser.

Everyone waited as he slid one end of the rope through the metal loop of the lock and secured the rope end to a floor nail with a bowline knot, which he had learned in sailing practice. He instructed Ranger to stand by the lock and lower it through the hole when told to do so.

Next, Chester threaded the pencil through the center of the round plastic piece so that it could twirl freely around the pencil. Dilly threw the blanket down through the hole and followed after it, skittering down the pipes inside the walls. He spread out the blanket and waited below. Chester grasped one end of the pencil with the tape-dispenser wheel centered midway, while Brown Bob lifted the eraser end. They laid it across the gaping hole in the floor where it rested secure, braced by both ends of the pencil. Brown Bob and Ranger watched as Chester draped the rope leading from the combination lock over the flat surface of the wheel created from the inside of the tape dispenser.

"What's that for, rodent?" Brown Bob whispered.

"The wheel will reduce the drag on the rope and make it easier for us when we lower the lock," Chester whispered back.

Ranger looked at Brown Bob and gestured toward Chester while tapping a claw behind one of his big ears. "The brain!"

Chester and Brown Bob clenched the long end of the rope tightly in their paws, while Ranger stood across from them on the opposite lip of the entry hole in the floor. At Chester's instruction Ranger pushed the lock to the edge, flattened onto his furry stomach, and gently lowered it into the dark abyss, holding onto the metal loop until he had to let go. Immediately Chester and Brown Bob were jerked forward by the yank on the rope they held when the weight of the lock dangled freely. Digging in their heels, they held tight, waiting for the swinging to stop. Chester had fashioned a simple pulley system. Slowly Chester and Brown Bob let the rope out, paw over fist, allowing it to slide easily over the wheel and the metal combination lock to drop slowly to the floor below. They heard Dilly's muffled squeak just as the tension on the rope eased. They had quietly and efficiently transferred the heavy weight ten feet without making a bit of noise.

Chester stood still at the hole, staring at his contraption, holding the rope in one paw while scratching his snout meditatively with the other.

"What's wrong, Ches?" Ranger asked.

"Nothing's *wrong*...I just realized that if we had *two* wheels, we could have lowered the lock more easily by winding the rope through both. Or—"

"Okay, okay, you can explain all that to me later…draw a picture or something. But right now let's get this lock safely into the room below."

Quickly they pulled the pencil away from the hole. Ranger picked the knot free from the nail, Chester tossed the loose rope to Dilly waiting patiently beneath them, and they all shimmied down the pipes to transfer themselves to the deck below.

The first light of dawn would soon be appearing. Mr. Cliff motioned for them to step it up. In silence they slid the lock into the back entrance of the human room and lifted it through the mouse hole into the closet.

Chester peeked into the interior of the room. He waited to make sure the way was clear. He could not hear a sound besides the heavy breathing of the sleeping midshipmen. A light shone from the hallway through the open door, making Chester blink. The humans were required to leave the doors to their quarters ajar at all times. The four mice, accompanied by Mr. Cliff, slid the blanket across the gleaming floor until it lay just under the gun locker, which had a swinging chain dangling from the handle. Chester motioned for the team to silently remove the cloth and then return to the safety of the closet.

This accomplished, he took one last look around the room. Everything was neatly stashed. Nothing in disarray. His gaze stopped at the blue trash can and lingered for a moment. Chester gave a little shudder and then glanced up at the bunk above the desk. Two brown eyes were gazing blearily at him. As the human rubbed his sleepy eyes, Chester took off at a run on all fours to the closet.

⚜

"I tell you, Briggs, I know it was a dream, but I could swear I saw that same mouse sitting on his hind legs staring up at me!"

A slant of early-morning sunshine cast a beam across the shiny gray floor of their dormitory room. Neither midshipman moved as they stood staring down at the silver and black combination lock resting in a patch of light near B. Wise's gun locker. Detailers made strident sounds in the hallway, but still they did not move.

"I wouldn't share that with anybody if I were you." T. Briggs looked his roommate in the eye. "About the mouse, I mean; they'll think you're crazy."

"I'm beginning to think I'm crazy. How did this get here?"

"Beats me." T. Briggs yawned. "I'm too tired to think about it. Maybe someone left it there as a joke."

"Some joke," B. Wise muttered as he picked up the lock. He opened a drawer in his desk and fished around for the folded paper with the number sequences to the locks sent by his parents. He twirled the dial on the heavy metal device three times, and the silver loop sprang open.

"It's mine." He gazed at his roommate in wonder.

## CHAPTER 19

# The End of Plebe Summer

❧

CHESTER STOOD OUTSIDE THE ENTRANCE hole to Bancroft Hall, saying good-bye to Mama, Papa, and a pawful of his many brothers and sisters. For security purposes they were not allowed to come any closer to the great gray stone building than the second crease in the pavement in front of the midshipmouse entry point. His little brother Bean continued to look with admiration at Chester in his clean white uniform. Mouse families clustered in little groups as they said good-bye with hugs, squeaks, pats, and sighs of encouragement to the plebe mice going back inside to continue training.

The night had been long but exciting and wonderful. Following the formal dress parade, Chester had been given free time with his family, time to sit and relax, which had felt so awkward. Chester squatted, but he kept looking over his shoulder to see if any detailers were bearing down on him to catch him in an infraction.

The plebe mice had even been allowed to leave the Yard and wander about the town outside the gates. It was their very first liberty, and most were given the official time off, unless they were on restriction. The only requirements were that they stay within a certain radius, a limited circle on a map, and remain in uniform at all times.

In the cobbled streets of Annapolis, Mama had followed Chester with a damp cloth in her paws, wiping his pristine white shirt and pants while he ate the treats they found. His favorite memory was when they had sat in an alley, gathered around a cardboard cup eating melted mint-chocolate-chip ice cream from a large white spoon held by Bean and Allie-Poo. Papa had peppered him with questions, while Mama adjusted the napkin tucked into his collar to protect his uniform, ready to dab at any green drips with her cloth.

Now it was dawn, and he had to be back for muster. Striding purposefully toward his wing, he joined up with the other plebe mice returning from their first taste of freedom after seven long weeks. Every mouse exuded a mixture of jovial celebration and inner tension. The parade had been the ceremonial end of Plebe Summer, a show for families and officials. But the mice still had to finish the last few days, and they knew it would not be made any easier. Reform would follow the end of the training period, and he wasn't sure what to expect. All he knew was that the older mid-shipmice would be returning from their summer assignments to resume studies, ready to make the lives of the plebe mice difficult. There would be even more upperclassmice crawling all over them, yelling their commands and expectations. The thirty companies would swell with the reappearance of the previous plebe class, now called *youngsters*, and the older second-class and first-class mice.

At the end of the hallway, he could see Dilly, who had already returned, preparing to lead them in their ritual singing of "Blue and Gold." He spied Ranger, who had his large head thrown back, laughing at the comment of another plebe mouse. His two large front teeth flashed in the dim light.

Chester felt refreshed but also a bit pensive following the last few hours of liberation from pressure and duty. His mind skimmed through the memories that had begun the moment they were awakened.

Even though it was a special night, they began with the usual evening PEP. Their detailers did not let up and ran the young rodents hard in the sweltering August heat. The plebe mice were excited to perform in the parade and see their families, so they did the exercises with renewed energy, their muscular bodies lean and taut after the seven long weeks of rigid training. One detailer warned them that if anyone fainted during the dress parade, they would not be able to participate in their first liberty and leave the Yard with their families.

After PEP, Chester and his nestmates had showered, polished their teeth, straightened whiskers, and trimmed the fur around their ears. Just as they were putting on their white works tunic and baggy pants for the last time, knotting the black ties around their necks and proudly wearing the midshipman cover with its shiny black brim and gold braid around the crown, Brown Bob sauntered into their quarters, confident and handsome.

Holding a paw over Chester's desk, he opened his claws, and a large silver *E* clattered onto the hard surface.

"What? Where did that come from?"

"That's for you, rodent. You saved my hide."

Chester stood silent, observing the compact mouse.

"Seems to me we work well together," he finally said in his quiet, deep voice.

Brown Bob flinched.

"Yeah, that's what Captain Thunder talked to me about. He made me see that...well, he talked about how everyone fails at some point here and that he had too. He told me that you wanted me on your team. I won't lie—there was a time when I wanted to be anything but on your team; now I would be the first to sign up to serve alongside you."

"Captain Thunder spoke to you?"

"Yeah, right before the Fisticuff Smoker. That was the clincher that made me decide not to leave. But I had already begun to rethink my decision after you came to my nest and told me I was a strong link in the chain. You didn't have to say that, but you did…and I had just got you dunked into a can. I thought about my brothers. They never told me about their failures; they only told me the good stuff."

"So what's with this?" Chester held up the immense *E* attached to a pushpin backing.

"I got that in the room below last night when we returned the metal weight. Looked around the closet, found it stuck into a ribbon bar over a shirt pocket, just like the ones we have on ours."

He pointed to Chester's summer white shirt, which was hung on a bent paper clip in his cubby, waiting to be worn for the first time after the parade. The multicolored rectangular bar pinned over the breast pocket sported two tiny, gleaming silver Es, representing his proficiency at the firing range.

"I thought you should have it." Brown Bob nudged the large metal *E* on the desk with a claw. "In appreciation."

Chester ducked his ears and looked sideways across the room at his nestmates, who became busy polishing their uniform parts and brushing imaginary dust from their black-brimmed covers.

"Thanks, Brown Bob," Chester replied gruffly. He stuck the silver letter *E* into the beam next to his desk. "Don't think I'll ever forget this summer."

The hallway erupted with the sound of trampling paws and flashes of white as members of their company dashed from their nests in their working white uniforms, tucking and twitching as they formed up at the bulkhead before they were led outside. Nearby they heard drumbeats stirring them to assemble into their companies, the shouts and calls of their company commanders, buglers warming up with toots, and even the whine of bagpipes.

After they were lined up, each company marched out with precision behind the flag bearers, their pretzel rifles held at perfect angles, glossy black eyes straight ahead, snouts turned toward the lead mouse at the end of the row, and covers tilted down at the perfect angle between their round ears. In the hot August night, they stood at attention as the companies were called, all thirty, to pass in review before the commandant, the superintendent of midshipmice, and the other visiting dignitaries. The heat was oppressive. Remaining motionless and standing at attention for so long required strength and discipline.

Lani said later that she had gotten a little woozy and almost passed out, which was strange because she was so tough. One mouse from Seventh Company did pitch forward and his limp body was dragged out of formation by his tail.

The plebe mice were marched quickly back to Bancroft Hall, where they scattered, with excitement, to their quarters. They quickly donned the pressed white uniform shirts with black shoulder boards and crisp creased pants. They cinched the white belts with shiny brass buckles around their middles and wiggled the ribbon bars over their left breast pockets with clean claws until they were perfectly straight. Ranger had an extra medal on his ribbon because he was prior enlisted. The three stood together in the entrance to their nest, ready to exit the building when commanded, and greet their families. They were proud to be wearing the midshipmouse dress white uniform for the first time.

Shrill scampered by in her pressed shirt and white skirt. She caught sight of the three nestmates and paused.

"Looking fine! Aren't you the Cheese! Hey, Pickle, you got a speck on your sleeve. Big rodent, what's your extra medal for? How did you rate? Hey, Chester, next time you get picked for a mission, how about asking me to go along?"

Shrill scurried off in a white blur.

"She called you Chester," Dilly commented.

"She called you Pickle," Chester replied.

"Pickle?" Ranger asked, his auburn brows drawn together over his round eyes.

"Dill," Chester and Dilly said together.

"Oh."

After the parade and changing into their new white summer uniforms, they reunited with their families on the long red-brick pathway leading away from Bancroft Hall. Mamas squeaked and cried; Papas slapped them on their backs and stared with admiration at their fine uniforms and signs of growth.

Grandfather stood among the throng of mice, a little apart from Chester's family, and waited until the greeting, backslapping, and hugging was over. Then he approached Chester, put his graying paw upon his shoulder, and looked into his eyes.

"You did it," he said. "I knew you would."

Chester nodded, narrowed his eyes, and honored Grandfather with a quick unofficial salute.

"Thank you, Grandfather, for everything."

"That's one-third down, two-thirds to go," Grandfather replied.

Chester blinked, wondering what that cryptic comment meant.

It all passed so quickly. Then Chester was back in the dormitory, detailers were shouting, and he was lined up against the bulkhead, at attention, two small silver Es gleaming on the ribbon above his pocket. As he awaited commands, his mind drifted back to the night when he realized he wanted to become a midshipmouse. He remembered the five midshipmice who visited his mouse household in the winter and how they had conversed confidently with

Grandfather. He had thought, *What would I look like in one of those uniforms?*

He glanced down at his dress whites to make sure his shirt was properly tucked in and the belt buckle was centered. He drew in his chin, stared straight ahead, and gave a little smile. At the end of the hall, he heard Dilly begin singing the first notes of the now familiar tune. His heart swelled as he joined in.

⚜

B. Wise proudly put on his crisp white shirt and creased white pants, centered the brass buckle of the belt, and knotted the laces of his perfectly polished white shoes. Glancing into the mirror, white cover with black brim tucked into his palm at his side, he gazed at the ironed shirt, especially the multicolored ribbon over his pocket. Eyes narrowed in disbelief, he erupted with a bellow heard through the rafters.

"Where is the *E* from my ribbon bar?"

Had he been listening quietly instead of yelling, he might have heard the strains of melody echoing in the rafters over his head:

*Now colleges from sea to sea*
*May sing of colors true;*
*But who has better right than we*
*To hoist a symbol hue?*
*For sailors brave in battle fair,*
*Since fighting days of old*
*Have proved the sailor's right to wear*
*The navy blue and gold.*

# GLOSSARY

**Annapolis:** Capital city of the state of Maryland. Situated on the Chesapeake Bay and the Severn River. Home of the United States Naval Academy.

**Bancroft, George:** US Secretary of the Navy. George Bancroft established the United States Naval Academy in Annapolis, Maryland, in 1845.

**Bancroft Hall:** The midshipmen dormitory. Construction of the building was begun in 1901. It now is the largest dormitory in the world and houses four thousand midshipmen.

**Battalion:** A grouping of multiple companies. Five companies comprise each battalion during the academic year.

**"Beat Army":** The response to "Go Navy!"

**Bearing:** Proper posture and facial expressions.

**Bilge:** To purposefully make yourself look better than someone else.

**Bill the Goat:** The Naval Academy mascot. A brass statue sits outside Lejeune Hall near the main gate into the academy.

**Brief:** A meeting where information is given.

**Brigade:** The entire body of midshipmen.

**Bulkhead:** Walls inside a building or a vessel.

**Camo:** Camouflage. Uniforms with patterns that allow the wearer to be indistinguishable from the background around them.

**Chiefs:** Senior enlisted members of the navy.

**Chop(ping):** Moving at double time through the center of hallways or in stairwells, pivoting around, or squaring corners with precision.

**Chow call:** A shouted compilation of information, including the weather, news reports, and entire menu for the day, down to the last detail.

**Color Company:** The company that has accumulated the most points in athletics, academics, parade, and military activities during a designated period.

**Company:** The group in which each midshipman lives and trains during his or her four years at the Naval Academy. There are thirty companies.

**Cover:** A white-crowned, shiny, black-brimmed hat with a yellow braid and gold anchor insignia.

**Dant:** Nickname for the commandant of midshipmen.

**Deck:** The individual floors in Bancroft Hall are called decks, much like different levels of a ship.

**Detailer:** An upper-class midshipman assigned to be a trainer for Plebe Summer.

**Eyes in the boat:** Eyes focused straight ahead.

**First class:** Fourth-year students, comparable to a senior.

**Formal dress parade:** Midshipmen march in companies, parade with rifles, respond to orders, and obey military commands in a regimented and ornamental fashion, accompanied by flag bearers, drums and bugles, and brigade leaders carrying swords. It is a part of training requiring discipline and teamwork.

**Fraternization:** An improper relationship (that is, it is against regulation to engage in a romance with a person in your company).

**Head:** Bathroom.

**Induction Day (IDay):** The day in late June or early July when all new plebes walk through the gates of USNA and take their oath. The first day of Plebe Summer. Equal in intensity to one-third of their time at the academy.

**Jones, John Paul:** Famous officer in the continental (Revolutionary War) navy. He was a skillful leader and hero known for saying, "I have not yet begun to fight!" His final resting place is in a beautiful marble-and-brass monument in the Naval Academy Chapel.

**King Hall:** The dining hall that feeds more than four thousand midshipmen at one time.

**Liberty:** Time off from regular duties with restrictions as to the distance one may travel.

**Man in the arena:** Words included in a speech by President Theodore Roosevelt that capture the essence of valor, honor, and glory in victory and defeat. Memorized by all plebes.

**Master chief:** Highest enlisted rank in the navy.

**Mother B:** Nickname for Bancroft Hall.

**"Navy Blue and Gold":** "Navy Blue and Gold" is the alma mater of the US Naval Academy. The words were composed by Commander Roy de Saussure Horn, USN (retired).

**Nimitz, Chester:** Chester and his grandfather were named after Chester Nimitz, who graduated from the US Naval Academy in 1905. He was an excellent student and athlete, who eventually earned the rank of fleet admiral in the US Navy.

**One-way hallway:** Usually as a disciplinary action, all plebes are required to travel in the same direction down a hallway, even if it means they must travel down to another deck and up the opposite staircase, chopping all the way, in order to visit the head on their own deck.

**PEP:** Physical education program.

**Plebe:** A first-year student at a military academy. The lowest in rank.

**Plebe Summer:** The boot camp, or intense-training segment, lasting six to seven weeks each summer for new Naval Academy students.

**Prior enlisted:** Having been a member of the military prior to acceptance to USNA.

**Professional knowledge:** Basic military information to be memorized.

**Rack:** Bed.

**Rack races:** A drill used by detailers to frustrate plebes and teach discipline. Beds are made with precision as quickly as possible and then ripped apart by trainers, only to be done all over again and again.

**Rates:** Required knowledge.

**Recon:** Reconnaissance. An expedition to gather information or, for the mice, supplies.

***Reef Points:*** The small blue instruction book issued to all plebes, containing information on tradition, mission, and history, most of which will be memorized by the end of the summer.

**Reform:** Time frame between the end of Plebe Summer and the beginning of the academic year. The upperclassmen return, and the brigade is reformed.

**Ribbon bar:** The multicolored bar worn over the left breast pocket.

**Separate:** To leave or be discharged from the military.

**SIQ:** Sick in quarters. Confined to sleeping quarters for medical reasons.

**Sir sandwich:** Beginning and ending each sentence with "sir."

**Supe:** Nickname for the superintendent of midshipmen.

**Tango Company:** Only in existence during Plebe Summer. The company for those plebes who express the desire to leave the academy. Counseling and time to reconsider are provided.

**Ward room:** A place containing recreational activities and refreshments for upperclassmen.

**White works:** The sailor working uniform.

**Winter dress blues:** Formal occasion attire. Dark pants and suit jacket with brass buttons, white shirt and tie, worn in the winter months.

**Yard, The:** The grounds of the Naval Academy. The gated 338-acre complex is a national historic landmark.

**Zodiac:** Large, rigid-hull, inflatable boats that hold several people.

CPSIA information can be obtained
at www.ICGtesting.com
Printed in the USA
LVHW022051011021
699240LV00018B/1616